A PLACE
NOT HOME

EVA WISEMAN

A PLACE
NOT HOME

Stoddart

*Stoddart Publishing gratefully acknowledges the support
of the Canada Council and the Ontario Arts Council in the
development of writing and publishing in Canada.*

First printed in 1996 by
Stoddart Publishing Co. Limited
34 Lesmill Road
Toronto, Canada M3B 2T6
(416) 445-3333

Canadian Cataloguing in Publication Data

Wiseman, Eva, 1947–
   A place not home

ISBN 0-7737-5834-8

1. Hungary — History — Revolution, 1956 — Juvenile fiction.
2. Refugees — Hungary — Juvenile fiction.   3. Refugees — Canada
— Juvenile fiction.   I. Title.

PS8595.I74P53   1996   jC813'.54   C96-930206-1
PZ7.W57P1 1996

Printed and bound in Canada

*For my mother and father
for making everything possible*

Acknowledgments
I want to thank my husband and children for their encouragement, support, and belief in me, and my sister who shared the adventure with me. I would also like to acknowledge the assistance of the Manitoba Arts Council and my gratitude to my editors, Kathy Lowinger and Anne Shone, for their infallible instincts and valuable advice.

Contents

1

Revolution

The sound of guns was deafening. Even covering my ears with my hands couldn't silence the continuous noise of machine-gun fire. We were all huddled under the big, round table in Father's office, at the front of our house. I put my arm around my sister, Ida, to feel her nearness and warmth. Mother clutched Father's hand so tightly that her knuckles turned white. Please God! Don't let us be shot! The taste of fear was sour in my mouth. The passing minutes bore the weight of eternity.

It was hard to believe it had been less than an hour ago that I had felt someone shaking my shoulders to waken me.

"Hurry up, Nelly! Get up! Be quick about it," said Mother, her voice high and tight with panic. I watched her bend over Ida, who had been snoring softly beside me.

"Why, what's the matter?" I asked. "What time is it?" Mother was anxiously wringing her hands.

"Is it morning already?" Ida asked through a yawn.

I was suddenly aware of a persistent banging outside the dark windows of our room. I couldn't place the noise. Was someone slamming a door very loudly over and over again? Was someone setting off firecrackers?

"I'll explain everything later," Mother said, handing us our robes and slippers. "Bring your blankets and pillows with you. We're going to sleep on the floor of Father's office tonight."

"What's going on?" I asked.

"Don't be frightened, girls." She tried to sound calm, but her fear was like a cloud around her. "I'll explain everything in a minute. Hurry up!"

Despite her words of reassurance, Ida and I were trembling. We followed her out of the room to Father's office, where she pushed us under the table. We watched Father's legs as he paced back and forth like a caged tiger.

"Listen to the guns, girls," Father exclaimed. "Remember this night. Never forget today's date— October 23, 1956. The unbelievable has happened. University students in Budapest are fighting the Communists. Hungary may become free once again. It's a miracle!"

"I am so scared!" Ida cried. "Why can't we sleep in our room?" Fear made her sound like a cranky baby, much younger than her eight years.

I was also tired, but reluctant to leave the shelter of the mahogany tabletop.

Father shouted to us above the roar of the machine-guns. "I heard on the radio that the Revolution has spread to Veszprem. There is shooting downtown."

"Oh my God! Are we going to be killed?" The blood was pounding in my ears.

"Hush, Nelly! You'll frighten your sister. There's probably nothing to worry about. But just to be on the safe side, Mother and I thought it would be a good idea for the whole family to camp down in my office tonight."

He spread out our blankets on the floor, and lay down on top of them. To see our father lying under the table like that suddenly seemed so funny that Ida and I burst out laughing as we went to join him. Our giggling Mother joined us. She soon stopped laughing, though, as the frightening chorus outside our windows became louder and louder with every passing moment. All we could do was cling together. The hours crawled by and we stayed huddled under the table, listening to the symphony of terror outside. At least we were still alive.

"Try to get some rest," Mother suggested to Ida and me.

"This stupid floor is so hard I won't sleep a wink all night," I complained, as if by whining I could make this awful night seem normal.

"Just close your eyes." Mother lay between us, and we curled up like kittens at her sides. Ida dropped off to sleep first. The stuffy smell of the carpet mixed with the scent of Mother's cologne was overpowering. My eyes got heavier and heavier, until a pounding on the door startled me back to wakefulness. Ida rolled over. Mother warned us not to make a sound. She covered us, even our heads, with the blanket. I wished I were invisible.

Father walked up to the door hesitantly. "Who is it?"

"It's Erno Gabor." Father let him in. I peeked out from under the blanket. Although the voice was familiar, I felt afraid even to breathe. Dr. Gabor's face was as white as snow; sweat was pouring off his brow. He looked very different from the last time he paid us a house call, when I had whooping cough.

"My God, Erno, are you ill? Kati, get him some brandy!"

"No, no, I'm okay. I must contact all the Jews in Veszprem. I've heard rumors that some of the former Nazis are making a list of the Jews who are left. They're planning a pogrom. They want to kill us all."

Mother muffled a cry of terror. Father was ashen. "This is unbelievable. Haven't we suffered enough? The war has ended."

"I must go," Dr. Gabor said. "I still have two more families to reach."

"What can I do to help?" Father asked.

"Everybody else has been told. There are so few of us left. Do you have a gun?"

"Of course not! I can't believe this is happening. What should we do?"

"I really don't know. We can only pray that it'll blow over. I'll contact you if I hear anything else." I heard the door quietly clicking open and then closed again.

I peeked out from under the blanket. Mother and

Father were looking at each other, neither one saying a word. They looked like statues, with all the life sapped out of their faces.

Father made the first move. "I'll get the ax from the shed. I hope to God I won't have to use it."

I had never seen him cry before. I couldn't bear to look. I turned onto my side, trying to find comfort on the hard floor. An exhaustion deeper than any I had ever known crept over me. I placed my hand under my head as a pillow, but my ring cut into my face. Amazingly, only a few weeks had passed since my birthday, when my parents had given it to me. It had become a part of me. Had I dreamed everything that had happened? But no, that was not possible. If I were dreaming, my ring wouldn't be hurting my face. I closed my eyes and the events of the past six weeks flooded my memory. I was back in my room, back in my bed, on a pleasant Sunday morning in September.

2

My Birthday

The warmth of the sun streaming through the lace curtains tickled my eyelids. Ida was still asleep beside me, her breathing heavy and even. The drapes cast a fiery shadow on her chubby cheeks. From outside, there was the neighing of a horse. Even though it was only eight o'clock on a Sunday morning, at least a dozen horse-drawn carriages carrying pigs, cows, hens, and roosters were already lined up outside our white-brick house. Father, the town veterinarian, regularly attended to his patients right on the street. It was often the horses themselves who required his attention. Ida and I were so used to the animal chorus that we barely noticed the neighing, barking, and crowing animals as we lay in our bed.

I was feeling deliciously drowsy. Ida sat up and stretched her arms, but I closed my eyes again, my thoughts drifting pleasantly over the day's lazy possibilities. Suddenly I remembered the date. Exactly one week from today—on September 9, 1956—I would be thirteen years old. Almost an adult. I could hardly believe it. I jumped out of bed. A thirteenth-birthday celebration is difficult to organize. Somehow I had to come up with an idea for a party that would dazzle my friends without upsetting my parents. That would be no easy task.

"Girls, come downstairs for breakfast." Mother's call broke through my thoughts. "I'd like your help in the garden this morning." My hopes for a lazy day evaporated.

I couldn't refuse to help because I hated to do anything to upset my mother, but it was harder to get along with her these days. She was having difficulty accepting that I was no longer a child. When I went anywhere with my friends, she cross-examined me about what we would be doing. And she humiliated me with my curfew, which was much earlier than any of my friends'. But I knew it was useless to complain because she would always say, "You have to understand, Nelly, that you and Ida are very precious to us. You're all we have left. We have to take very good care of you."

I was so tired of hearing this. I knew the reason as well as I knew my own name. All of our family, my grandparents, aunts, uncles, and cousins were killed by the Germans during the war. I knew how Mother was able to save me by giving me to the nuns from the convent that used to be on top of the hill. The nuns hid me for two years. I was only a baby, but the story of how I was kept safe was as much a part of me as my arm. Once I tried to explain to Mother that I didn't really want to hear so much about my dead relatives because I couldn't remember them anyway, but she said that it was my duty to keep their memory alive. She became very angry when I tried to tell her that if I was mature enough for such a responsibility I should be trusted to come home after eight o'clock at night. Then she began to cry, and I wished that I could take back my hurtful words.

It wasn't always like this. When I was younger, I would pour my heart out to Mother over countless cups of hot cocoa. But gradually, as I got older, we stopped talking to each other. She still told me to clean up my room or do my homework, and other motherly things, but we never seemed to say anything important to each other anymore. Mother complained that I didn't talk to her as I used to. I wondered why I would, though, when she would only criticize me. But sometimes I missed the closeness we had shared. My friends told me I was lucky to have a mother who was so nice and who really understood me. But, somehow, I began to feel that Mother's interest was an invasion of my privacy, and that she was so hopelessly old-fashioned.

Mother probably expected me to celebrate my birthday by inviting the usual group of girls for birthday cake, so I knew I had to convince her that this year was different. But Mother was strict, and money was scarce. Besides, the stores were only carrying the most basic things these days.

As I worked in the garden, my thoughts kept turning to the party, but it wasn't until late afternoon that I had time to myself. I went to my room, sprawled comfortably in my armchair, and settled down to planning. I needed my best friend, Sari. She, more than anybody else, understood the importance of a good plan. Sari and I walked to school together every day. We sat beside each other in classes, and we walked home together at the end of the day.

Most often, Sari came to my house. I didn't like visiting her because her apartment was so terribly over-crowded. She had to share a room with her fifteen- and sixteen-year-old sisters, Edith and Zsuzsi. They were always having friends over, curling their hair or making up their faces. Poor Sari! Compared to Mrs. Weiszman, Mother was an angel. Sari was always being thrown out of her own room because her mother claimed that Edith and Zsuzsi needed their privacy—as if Sari didn't! When she came over to our house, we could usually have my room to ourselves. Ida was such a tomboy that she preferred to be outdoors climbing trees or playing tag.

The moment I thought of her, Sari appeared in the doorway. Her timing couldn't have been better.

"We've got to decide what to do for my birthday this year," I said by way of greeting her.

Sari did her usual tour of my room before she answered. She loved my room. I understood her feelings. Even though my room was tiny, it was my favorite spot in the whole world. The tall windows, the white-washed walls, the parquet floor covered by a threadbare gold-and-green carpet, faded to a nice mellow color, and the forest-green sofa that became the bed I shared with Ida at night felt like home to me. In front of the lace-curtained windows stood a round table, also lace-covered, flanked by two green armchairs. These were the only things left from the grand house my parents had owned before the war. The rest was gone. Mother had crocheted a golden afghan for the sofa to hide the stain left by the bottle of ink I once spilled on the armrest. Crowded shelves on the walls held my favorite books by my favorite author, Jules Verne, and my shell and rock collections, which I dusted every day. A huge wood-burning ceramic stove in the corner kept the room warm and cozy during the winter.

Finally, Sari threw herself down into the other arm-chair with a faraway look in her eyes. "Why don't we go tobogganing? It would be so romantic! I can just imagine you gliding down the snow-covered hills behind Miki, your scarf trailing behind you." She sighed.

Sari was a true romantic, and my opposite in every way. While I was practical, she was idealistic; I was talk-ative, and she was quiet; I was a bookworm, but she wouldn't pick up a book unless she absolutely had to. Even our appearances were very different. She was short, with straight, white-blond hair and dimples. It was difficult to see her skin under the thick covering of freckles she had tried to fade, without much success, with lemon juice. I thought they were rather pretty, but I couldn't convince her to leave them alone. She loved my dark, curly hair, which I wore in braids to straighten it. Most of all, I was jealous of how much Sari could eat.

Nobody could eat like her—jelly doughnuts, fried pota-toes, every fattening food imaginable. Yet she never gained weight while I, who ate cucumber salads and sensible soups, looked like a walking pillow. Sari was the most loyal girl I had ever known, and she knew that she could always count on me, too. Her only fault was her sense of romance. This time, even I was surprised by her. Tobogganing in September!

"What are you talking about? It won't snow for months. You can't toboggan without snow." Why did I have to explain this to her?

"Maybe we could pray for snow," Sari said with a giggle.

"Don't be silly! We have to think of something else. But what's the use? Miki doesn't even know I'm alive. Why should he bother with me when every girl in the whole school has a crush on him?"

I knew that Sari would never tell my secrets to anybody, even under torture. She was the only person in the whole world who knew how much I liked Miki. Miki was the smartest and most handsome boy in grade nine, and the school's top soccer player. Best of all, he was the only boy who was taller than me.

"Why shouldn't Miki like you?" Sari said loyally. "You have beautiful brown eyes, a great personality, and you're the smartest girl in grade seven."

"Who cares about school? I wish I looked like Jutka. Then Miki would like me."

That wasn't completely honest. I liked school and was proud of my reputation as the class brain. But I did envy Jutka Kocsis her blond hair and blue eyes. To make

12

things worse Jutka, and just about all of my friends except Sari, had developed what Mother called a "womanly figure". When I once suggested to Mother that maybe something was wrong with me, she laughed and told me to be patient, that "my time" would come. But when? When would I lose my puppy fat? When would I stop tripping over my own two feet? When would I know what to say to boys? And, most importantly, when would I get breasts? It was obvious that a series of miracles would have to occur before a boy like Miki could like me. But I never gave up hope, and neither did Sari. Finally, she came up with a wonderful plan.

"Why don't you have a dance . . . with boys! I know that's what Zsuzsi wants to do on her birthday."

"You're a genius! I could invite Miki, and maybe he'd even ask me to dance." I imagined myself elegantly dressed in a beautiful dress that showed off my "womanly figure", twirling around the dance floor in Miki's arms to the strains of haunting violin music. Miki would ask me to be his girlfriend, confess his love for me, and beg me to marry him. My daydream bore a close resemblance to the plots of the novels I regularly stole from the bookshelf by Mother's bed. As always, the thought of Mother snapped me back to reality. "Mother will never let me ask boys! She doesn't realize that I'm not a child anymore."

"You've got to convince her somehow, Nelly. It's the opportunity of a lifetime." Sari looked at her watch. "I'd better go home or I'll be late for supper. See you tomorrow morning."

I immediately went to the kitchen to find Mother. She was cooking dinner.

"Let me help," I offered. "I'll shell the peas." They plopped with a hard ring as she emptied them into a metal bowl.

She lifted her eyes to the ceiling suspiciously in response to my offer. But I knew from past experience that it would be foolish of me to explain, so I just smiled and took the bowl away from her.

"So, Nelly," she said, wiping her hands on a dish towel, "what's going on?"

"Nothing, really. I just wanted to see if you needed some help. By the way, next week's my birthday." I tried to sound nonchalant. "Sari thinks I should have a dance." I continued to shell the peas.

There was a long silence. I looked up. Mother's eyes were bright and her lips were trembling, as if she wanted to laugh. "A party with boys?" she asked.

"Of course with boys! You can't have a dance without boys." Even to my own ears I sounded too defensive.

Mother was quickly losing the battle with her lips. I could feel the heat rising in my cheeks. I was so certain she wouldn't give me her permission that I almost missed her smile. Instead, she asked, "What can I do to help?"

Could I be hearing properly? A dance! None of my friends had ever had boys to their birthday celebrations. I'd be the first one!

"Do you still want a family dinner before the party?" Mother asked. Ever since I could remember she had always cooked the birthday girl's favorite dishes.

I threw my arms around Mother's neck. "I wouldn't miss my dinner for anything!"

"There's only one problem," she said. "This year your birthday falls on Sunday, just three days after Rosh Hashanah. Sunday afternoon is the only time Father can leave his practice to come with us to the cemetery. We'll have to prepare everything that morning before we go."

Every year, between the New Year and Yom Kippur (the Day of Atonement eight days later), we visited the Jewish cemetery on the outskirts of town. Only Great-Grandfather Kohn was actually buried there. There were no graves for those murdered by the Nazis in concentration camps, but Mother and Father had had a gravestone erected with the names of our family members who had perished inscribed on it. It may sound morbid, but I liked visiting the cemetery. It was a beautiful place, full of trees. All of our relatives were killed when I was a baby, but whenever I was in the cemetery I felt close to them, as if I had known them. Although I was worried we wouldn't have time to get ready for my party, I knew there was no choice. I would never have asked Mother to let me stay at home.

Sari rang my doorbell at quarter to eight the next morning. Both of us were dressed in dark skirts, knee socks, white blouses, and the crimson Young Pioneers' neckerchiefs that identified members of the Communist youth group. There was to be a meeting after school. All of our friends belonged. Even though membership wasn't compulsory, our teachers and principal made it clear that we were expected to join.

"So, what did your mother say about the dance?" Sari asked, shifting her briefcase from one hand to the other. Our teachers were very generous with homework.

"You're not going to believe it, but she loved the idea. Now we've got to decide who we're going to invite."

Suddenly we heard somebody shouting behind us. "Hey, Nelly, Sari, wait up! What's the big rush?"

"Oh my God! It's Miki and he wants to walk with us."

"I told you he likes you," Sari whispered.

"Hush! He'll hear you. Oh no! He's got Sam Gabor with him." I'd disliked Sam ever since he made fun of me in the fifth grade by chanting "Nelly, Nelly, she has a fat belly!" When I once asked Miki how he could be such good friends with Sam, he said that Sam only acted strangely around me. Sari insisted that Sam had a secret crush on me.

"We've been talking about you boys," Sari said with a giggle. "Nelly is trying to decide whether to invite you to her birthday party."

"Stop it, Sari! Of course they're invited. I hope you'll both come. It's next Sunday at seven o'clock."

"We'd love to. Wouldn't we, Sam?"

Sam was smiling smugly. "I guess so. You're becoming boy crazy, Nelly. Just like all the other girls in our class."

"How dare you! Why I——"

"Come on, you two. Stop it!" Miki was laughing, while behind his back Sari was making faces to shut me up.

By this time, we had climbed the small hill to our school. It was the same building where the nuns had hidden me during the war, but the nuns were gone now. After the Russians occupied Hungary, they had converted the convent to a school. The rambling building stood at the edge of a thick woods. Some of the leaves on the trees were already turning to fiery autumn colours. The morning bell rang to mark the beginning of the school day as we entered through the heavy wooden doors. Miki and Sam went to their home room, and Sari and I to the grade seven classroom.

"What's the matter with you?" Sari whispered in my ear as we settled into our desks. "Why can't you get along with Sam? Do you want Miki to think you're a baby? For a minute, I thought you were going to hit Sam."

"I *was* going to! He infuriates me more than anybody else in the whole world."

"He isn't so bad," Sari said. "You're overreacting. I told you that he likes you a lot. That's why he's so silly around you."

The stately entrance of our home room teacher, Mr. Kelen, cut off my reply.

"Everybody must be on time tomorrow morning," he announced. "Four horse-drawn buggies are being sent at eight o'clock to take us to the collective farm. We'll spend the day helping our farmer comrades care for their livestock. Thanks to the efforts of our new First Secretary of the Communist Party, Comrade Gero, the farm is flourishing and our comrade farmers are happy and prosperous. Let's clap to honor Comrade Gero." And he led us to clap in rhythm as we chanted: "Long live Gero! Long live Gero!" I glanced at Sari on my left. She looked back at me and rolled her eyes but, like the rest of us, she was clapping enthusiastically in Comrade Gero's honor. Mr. Kelen's eyes scanned the room to see if any of the students lacked the proper zeal.

"Pack up your books," he said when we had finished. "Mrs. Horvat is waiting for you in Russian class."

I was among the last people to leave the classroom. I rushed out without looking and carelessly knocked into the door frame. All my books spilled from my arms onto the hall floor. Tibor Szabo turned back to help me. As we were crouching on the floor gathering everything up, I noticed an uncharacteristically grim frown on his good-natured face.

"What's the matter with you?"

Tibor was biting his lips angrily. "Liars," he spluttered, "bloody liars. Not a word of what they're saying is true. 'Happy and prosperous comrade farmers.' Ridiculous! The farmers are miserable. My grandpa is one of them, so I know. The government took his land away from him. Now he works for almost nothing. I'd like to——"

"Hush! Don't say another word! Sylvia Kapus just turned the corner. You know that she is an informer."

Tibor nodded with a set face. "Never believe what they tell you," he muttered.

"I know, I know! My parents say the same thing." And I pushed him into the Russian room before he could say anything foolish to Sylvia.

I didn't want to be responsible for Tibor or his grandfather receiving a visit in the middle of the night from the secret police, the AVO. I would never forget how my friend Rozsi Nagy's father had disappeared last year. Rozsi didn't come to school for a week and, when she finally did return, her eyes were red and swollen. Nobody knew what was wrong with her, and Rozsi wouldn't tell us. We found out what had happened when Sari overheard two of our teachers discussing how Mr. Nagy was transported to Siberia for criticizing the government. No one ever heard from him again.

For the first time in my life I was happy to be in Russian class, listening to Mrs. Horvat drone on and on about Russian verbs. At least she took my mind off Tibor's anger. Soon I was even able to shut out her high-pitched voice and daydream about something more important—my birthday party. Just six more days to go!

During the next week I was busy planning my birthday dance. Finally, the day arrived. I checked my watch over and over again on the way to the cemetery. It was only three o'clock in the afternoon, and everything for my party was ready and awaiting our return home. Even the table was set with the few mismatched pieces of fine bone china Mother was able to recover after the war. Salty rolls, flavored butter, vegetables, and peaches, which had been given to my father by a grateful farmer, were covered with embroidered cloths in the cool pantry. In just four hours I would have my first party with boys! Father left the car outside the cemetery gates and we entered on foot.

"My God! What's happened?" I asked when I looked around me. The cemetery was wrecked. It looked as if a gigantic hurricane, an evil force, had destroyed it. The headstones were thrown about in all directions. Some blocked the paths between the graves, and several were broken into pieces. Only a small corner of Great-Grandpa Kohn's headstone had chipped off. The colorful flowers, which usually gave the cemetery such a peaceful appearance, were uprooted, the blossoms crushed. It was strange how their fragrance still perfumed the air. The graves had been trampled. There were imprints of large boots on the sod. Most frightening of all were the sinister black swastikas painted over all the headstones. Father had taken a white handkerchief out of his pocket and was trying to rub away the one on Grandfather Kohn's stone, but it wouldn't come off. Mother knelt at the foot of the grave, staring into space, her hands still and open in her lap. Ida realized something was wrong and began to cry. I remembered with a chill that I had seen those swastikas before, a long time ago. Ida asked Father what they were.

"Swastikas, symbols of the damned Nazis." Father raged. "The bastards! Is it never enough for them?"

My heart was pounding, my hands clammy with fear. I read my terror in Father's eyes and on Mother's face. What was happening? The Nazis had killed the Jews during the Second World War; that's why I had no grandparents, aunts, uncles, or cousins. Only Mother, Father, and Ida. Had the Nazis come back to kill the rest of us?

Father tried to straighten Grandfather's gravestone. I helped him. We pushed with all of our strength. The muscles in my arms and legs were straining, as if they would snap at any moment. We pushed and pushed, until the stone was finally upright. I ran my fingers over the cold marble and caressed the names carved into it. These weren't mere names to me. They were my family, my link to the past. A chill ran down my spine when I read the name Karolina Adler inscribed near the top of the stone. She was my grandmother, and she was a bookworm like me. Aaron Adler's name was right below hers. He was my grandpa, and he loved animals as much as my father did. Father told me that he had always kept five dogs at his country home. Farther down was Nusi Weisz, my aunt, the family beauty. I thought Mother must have been joking when she told me I looked just like her.

I crouched down and tried to smooth out the trampled grass over the grave with my hands, but the damage was too great. I couldn't put back the geraniums, but at least I could gather up the fragrant petals and lay them around the grave. They were blood-red against the grass. "This is going to ruin my birthday," I told myself while working on my knees. Immediately, I was truly ashamed. What kind of a person was I, to think of myself at a time like this?

Father knelt down beside Mother and whispered to her. She was still staring into space. He wrapped his arms around her and helped her up to the car. I followed with Ida, who was clinging to me, crying. The ride home was so quiet. I could hear the rolling car wheels beating out a strange tune against the dirt road, as if they were saying over and over, "Are the Nazis coming back? Are the Nazis coming back?" I looked at Father's face. His jaw was set and his expression was stony. But, finally,

Mother was coming back to life. When we got home she seemed surprised that the table was already set.

"Oh no—your birthday party," she said. "I completely forgot. Your friends will be here soon."

"The party has to be postponed," Father said.

"Father's right!" I heard myself say. "I don't feel like celebrating anymore." I avoided Father's eyes to hide my guilty thoughts—what would my friends, especially Miki, think about me if I called off my birthday party at the last minute?

Mother's face was lined with worry. "Oh, I don't know if it's right to cancel on such short notice. . . ."

"I have to disagree with you, Kati. None of us is in a party mood anymore," Father said. "You have my word, Nelly, that we'll have your party as soon as possible, but it's out of the question to have it today." Both Mother and I knew that it was useless to argue with Father when he used such a firm tone.

"Believe me, dear, your friends will understand. They must all know what's happened by now. We'll still have our family dinner, and Father and I will give you your gifts." I think Mother was trying to console both me and herself.

Father was already telephoning all his friends, many of whom also had relatives buried in the cemetery. Slowly, I wheeled my bike out of the shed and rode to each guest's house. I told them my party was canceled because Mother wasn't feeling well. Somehow, I couldn't bring myself to talk about the real reason.

* * *

Dinner was at six o'clock. Except for being a little pale, Mother was her usual self. All of my favorite foods were waiting for me—tender mashed potatoes, cucumber salad with paprika seasoning, and a goose, roasted to a deep brown. A farmer whose horse Father had treated had had no money to pay him and settled his veterinary bill with the goose. We were more fortunate than many of our neighbors for the farmers often paid Father with meat and butter, which were very difficult to get. Mother was always frightened that Father would get into trouble with the police over such illegal payments, but she was still happy to use whatever he brought home. It was difficult to run a household without such basic necessities as oil, lard, and paper, in addition to meat and butter. Although she was young, Ida realized that she must never breathe a word to anyone about Father allowing the farmers to pay for his services in such a way.

Father always opened a bottle of homemade wine on special occasions. Usually, Ida and I were only allowed to have soda water but, in honor of my birthday, Father poured a little wine into my glass. Even Ida drank a thimbleful. It tasted good, and it made my head feel light. Both Ida and I started to laugh. Father raised his glass in a toast.

"To a very fine daughter! May all your dreams come true," he said, and hugged me. Mother kissed me. They had three packages for me, one large, one medium-sized, and one very small. All three were wrapped in brown paper. I shook the largest package, which felt light, then tore off the paper as fast as I could. Inside, was the most beautiful party dress I had ever seen—soft, navy blue

23

velvet with a white lace collar and cuffs. I recognized the material right away. Mother had made over her only party dress for me. When I was little, I used to stroke the material to feel how soft it was. The new dress would have been perfect for my party. I was to have worn my old sailor dress, which was nice, but two years old and tight under the arms, even though Mother had let it out. This dress was so pretty. I was sure Miki would have been impressed by it.

"Oh, it's such a beautiful dress! How did you know it's exactly what I wanted?" I asked Mother.

"You hinted enough, Nelly!" It was so good to hear Mother laughing again. "I wish we could have bought you a brand-new dress, but there is so little clothing in the stores."

"It's perfect! I wouldn't want another one."

"Aren't you forgetting something?" Father asked Mother. She handed me the medium-sized package. It was even lighter than my first gift.

"Be careful when you unwrap it," she warned me as I unrolled a pair of gossamer nylon stockings with a brown seam running down the back of each leg. My first pair ever! They were so delicate I was afraid even to breathe on them.

"How were you ever able to find such a fine pair?" I asked Mother. "They must be from America!" Hungarian nylon stockings were much thicker and rougher in texture.

Mother was smiling complacently. "You're quite right, Nelly. Mrs. Lovas's family in America sent them to her, and she traded them with me for a kilogram of butter." I knew Mother could have used the butter herself, which made me appreciate the gift even more.

"Now for your last gift," Father said, and he handed me the smallest package. I unwrapped a beautiful gold signet ring with my initials, "K. A.", for Kornelia Adler. I was actually speechless for a moment, which was a rare occurrence. Father slipped the ring onto the fourth finger of my right hand. It fit perfectly, as if it had been made for me.

"Wear it every day," Mother said.

"It belonged to my mother, who had the same initials as you," Father told me. "It's the only thing I was able to get back after the war."

"I swear I'll never take it off my finger."

"It's something you'll have for the rest of your life; something to remember your parents by, even when you're grown up." I was surprised by how emotional Father sounded. His voice was choked with tears.

"I have something for you, too," Ida announced. From behind her chair she brought out a pair of bright red mittens. The right thumb was slightly bigger than the left. "I knitted them myself," she said, looking at Mother who was nodding her approval.

"They're beautiful, Ida. I really need a pair for tobogganing." I kissed her round face, and she giggled with pleasure.

After we had finished dinner, Mother brought out a bowl of peaches.

"I know we're celebrating your birthday, Nelly, but I think we should take a few minutes to talk about what happened at the cemetery," Father said seriously.

"We're so sorry that you had to see something like that," Mother said with a sigh.

Ida, who had been sitting quietly, raised her head. "They broke the stones," she said in a whisper. The warmth around the table vanished.

"Why would somebody vandalize a cemetery like that? Who could be so wicked?" I hated the way my voice was quavering.

"Both of you girls know that our families were killed during the war," Father said.

"Vili, please——" Mother was wringing her hands. I hated to see her so unhappy. Ida buried her face in Mother's shoulder and was mute.

"The children have to remember, Kati," Father said. "Ida is still very young, but it's important for both of them to understand."

"I understand, Father," I told him. "But the war ended eleven years ago. Who would vandalize the cemetery now?" I still couldn't control my voice.

"I don't know, Nelly. Even today many people are full of hate."

Ida had started humming quietly to herself to shut him out. I felt as if a dam had opened up and my words came pouring out. "But why? What did you or Mother or I or Ida ever do to them? Why do they want to hurt us? Why did they kill your parents and our other relatives during the war?" The moment the words tumbled out of my mouth I realized these were questions that I had wanted to ask them for a long time, but I had always been afraid to in case they hurt my parents.

"I don't know why," Father answered. "Hungary fought on Germany's side in the war, and when the Jews were deported to concentration camps by the Germans, the Hungarian government took away—stole—our properties. All of our things, our furniture, our clothes, even our houses, were given to Hungarian Nazi sympathizers. When some of us surprised them by surviving the death camps and returning home, these Nazi sympathizers had to return our property to us. Many of them are angry to this day."

Father looked exhausted, as if he had tried to explain these things to himself many times. I looked away from him, hating to see the sad expression in his eyes. "Do you understand what I am saying, Nelly, Ida?"

Ida was still clinging to Mother's neck. She ignored him. How could he expect us to understand such hatred? "Why don't we call the police? If somebody breaks the law you should always call the police. Maybe they could catch these criminals. Surely the police would help us?" I asked him.

"What could the police do? There are too many of these villains, and only a few of us. We'd only be calling attention to ourselves. Who knows what they might do next? The best thing we can do is ignore them. It's very important to remain inconspicuous. Always remember that! Then maybe they'll forget about us and leave us alone."

A wave of fury engulfed me. I banged my fist on the table, but I was so angry that I felt no pain. "It's not fair! They shouldn't get away with it!"

Father patted my face softly. He avoided my eyes.

"No, it's not fair. But there's very little we can do about it."

"It's not fair," I repeated. "How can you just accept it?" I was so angry that I couldn't look at him.

"I don't accept it, Nelly, and I can't tell you why people commit such horrible acts. Our main concern is to stay together, and to stay safe," Father said. "But enough serious talk. After all, today is a big day for you."

Mother jumped up, rushed out of the room, and returned with a beautiful Dobos torte she had baked for me. The cake had five chocolate layers and a glazed candy topping. Thirteen lighted candles formed a circle around my name, which Mother had written on the top.

"Make a wish, make a wish!" Ida cried.

I closed my eyes and wished really, really hard, for I had two wishes. I wished for the Nazis never to come back, and I wished for Miki to like me.

Later that night I went into the kitchen to say good night to Mother. She was sitting in the kitchen staring at a small box on the table in front of her. I had seen the contents of this box many times. It contained three photographs wrapped in tissue paper. They were the only pictures of her family that Mother was able to recover after the war. The first one was a formal portrait of my great-grandparents. Great-Grandfather Kohn had a magnificent handlebar mustache. He stood very straight and proud in the uniform he wore to fight in the Hungarian army during the First World War. Beside him sat my great-grandmother, staring calmly into the camera. She was prim and proper in a high-necked lace blouse, with her hair swept into a glossy topknot. The second picture showed my mother's father, my grandfather. He was sitting on the ground in a wooded area, surrounded by a group of disheveled men. They were all wearing heavy clothing and peaked military-style caps. This picture was taken in 1943 after my grandfather was conscripted into a forced-labor regiment of Jews to build roads in Yugoslavia. Mother unwrapped the pictures and picked up the largest of the three photographs, the one I liked the best. This picture showed her parents, still young, and my mother as a fat little girl. She was holding her father's hand, and was laughing and looking up at her mother, who was dressed in a long, black coat with a fur boa. Even though the picture was in black and white, I knew somehow, by the utterly happy expression on my mother's face, that the sun must have been shining that day.

Mother was staring at this photograph with a faraway look in her eyes and a half smile on her lips. I had a feeling that she couldn't really see the picture, or me standing there. I tiptoed out of the kitchen.

3

My Party

For weeks I didn't feel like having a birthday party at all, but then I started thinking that that would mean I had let those hateful vandals win. From that moment, I began to plan seriously. The party would take place on October 23.

My friends had promised to be at my house by seven o'clock in the evening, but Sari had arrived early to help get everything ready. We pulled apart the tall white doors separating the living and dining rooms. It took a lot of effort to roll up the carpets, exposing the hardwood floors for dancing. We made room for precious records beside the phonograph in the corner. Sari hung colorful crêpe-paper streamers on the ceramic stove and the windowsills. It was lucky that Father was at home to help us pull the dining-room table to the wall. It was so heavy that we wouldn't have been able to budge it without him. We set the table with food and fruit punch. Mother was proud that she had been able to get the ingredients for another cake. It was to be brought in all lit with birthday candles later on.

By seven o'clock it was already dark. I was wearing my new velvet dress and stockings. The gold ring glistened on my finger. Sari had pulled my hair into a ponytail, a more grown-up hairstyle than braids. I bit my lips to make them redder before looking in the mirror. I must admit, I looked rather nice.

"Pretend there's a book on your head," Sari commanded. She had read in a magazine that if you practice walking with a book on top of your head, you'll glide like a fashion model. The whole idea seemed ridiculous to me, but I humored her by sucking in my stomach and lifting my chin. "Much better," Sari said, looking me over. "You look fantastic! At least fifteen."

All of my girlfriends arrived a few minutes later, but none of the boys. The girls admired my new dress and gold ring. I could sense that they were envious of my stockings. Everybody gave me gifts. From Sari, a large tin of peanuts, my favorite treat. I also liked Eva Klein's present, a leatherbound diary with a lock and key. Agi Kovacs brought me the book *Twenty Thousand Leagues Under the Sea* by Jules Verne.

The girls kept asking when the boys would be arriving. It was getting late, and I began to worry. What if all the boys had decided not to come? But soon the doorbell rang, and all eight of them arrived together. Miki and Sam were among them.

"Happy birthday, Nelly," Miki said, handing me a box of candy, each piece wrapped in different colored shiny paper. He had a huge smile on his face. It was the first time ever a boy had given me a gift. "It's a beautiful party. Thank you for inviting me."

"I'm very happy you could come." No matter how hard I tried, I couldn't think of anything else to say.

Sam gave me his gift, a board game with four different games to play on it. His ears were bright red. I forced myself to smile as I thanked him.

All the boys were clustered on one side of the room, shoving each other and joking around. Mother, who was in and out of the room, was unsuccessful in getting them to dance with us.

"Maybe if I danced with you, the rest of them would start," I suggested to Sari. I put on a record, took Sari's hand and, though I towered over her, we began to waltz. I felt like a fool dancing with another girl, but Ida and Eva followed our example. Soon all the girls were dancing with each other, while the boys stood by the wall, their eyes fixed on their feet. Sari put on a jazz record. I was whirling her around the dance floor, when I felt a tap on my shoulder.

"Would you like to dance?" Miki asked. He was biting his lower lip and rocking on his heels. Somehow this relaxed me.

"Of course, I'd love to dance," I answered, trying out my most mysterious smile. Secretly, I wiped my wet palms on the back of my dress.

Miki and I concentrated on our feet for a few minutes, not saying anything to each other. I tried to appear as if dancing with the boy of my dreams was an everyday occurrence. "You're the prettiest girl here, Nelly," Miki whispered suddenly. "Do you think you could come for a walk with me sometime? We could go to the patisserie for ice cream."

I closed my eyes, wanting the moment to last forever. He liked me! "I'd love to! When?" I thought I should fix the date before he changed his mind.

"What about next week, on Sunday afternoon? I'll phone you in the morning to arrange a time."

"That sounds wonderful," I managed to reply in a calm voice. I hoped Mother would let me go. Me! Me! Me! My heart sang. He liked me!

The rest of the evening I was swimming in a kaleidoscope of color, of music, of laughter, of pleasure. Me! Me! Me! He liked me! I kept repeating the refrain to myself, my secret too precious to share even with Sari. I was certain that everybody noticed my happiness; I couldn't stop smiling. But I guess they all thought that I was just enjoying my birthday party.

By eleven o'clock the party was over. I was tired, but in the pleasant way that followed a perfect day. Mother told us to leave the cleaning up until the next morning. After we changed into our pyjamas, Ida and I went to say good night to our parents in Father's office. We used it as a den in the evenings. Mother and Father were sitting by the radio, listening intently to the announcer.

"Good night, Mother! Good night, Father! I had the

greatest birthday party of my entire life. And I got some nice presents. Wasn't it the best party you've ever seen?"

"We'll talk about it tomorrow, dear," Mother said, giving us each a quick hug. Father merely waved us out of the room. Tiny cold fingers of fear tore away at the warm feeling left by the party. My parents always chatted with us every evening before bed, discussing how we had spent the day. But tonight they hardly seemed to notice us. What was wrong?

A sudden loud burst of gunfire startled me back to reality. I was no longer remembering my birthday, no longer eating my mother's Dobos torte, even though I could almost taste its sweetness on my tongue. I was no longer laughing with my friends at my party or bidding my parents good night afterward. What I was doing instead was cowering under a table, on the floor of Father's office, in the middle of a violent revolution. My heart was beating in my throat for I was afraid that any minute we would be killed by machine-gun fire. Was it really only a few hours ago that I had been twirling on the dance floor with Miki?

4

Captured

Mother was sitting beside me on the piano bench while I practiced the piano. Even my own ears told me that I was playing in the wrong key. Mother's eyes were fixed on the music, but she didn't seem to hear me. My grandmother had been a piano teacher, and both Mother and Ida had inherited her musical talent. But me! I must have taken after Father's side of the family. All his relatives were tone deaf. Mother insisted that I practice for a half hour every day. She said that I would be grateful I had when I was grown up. I continued to miss notes, but still got no response from Mother.

I didn't mind practicing—it gave me something to do. It was already November 7 and school had been cancelled for the past fifteen days, since the Revolution had broken out. A week ago the Russian soldiers reoccupied our city. The Revolution had failed. The last week had been unbearably boring. A strange lethargy had overcome us.

One day, for a change, I took Ida to look at the cannons and tanks parked in front of the Russian headquarters. The military equipment was so interesting to see that we were a half hour late getting home for supper. We were surprised to find our anxious parents waiting for us at the end of our street. Father was furious and Mother had tears in her eyes.

"Where were you? We've called all of your friends and nobody knew where you went," Father cried.

"We went to see the Russian tanks," I explained in my most reasonable tone.

"Are you crazy? To put yourself and your sister into such danger!" Father thundered. "Who knows what those Russians might do? How could you cause us such anxiety? Stay away from the Russians in the future! And that's an order!"

"I knew something was wrong," Mother said.

"But Mother, we were only a few minutes late!"

"That doesn't matter!" Mother replied. "In the future, try to think before you act. We couldn't bear it if anything happened to you or Ida. You are all Father and I have."

You'd think by the way they were acting that we had gone for a ride in the tanks instead of just looking at them from across the street. At first I was angry, but almost immediately guilt made me feel nauseous. I hated to make my parents frightened. They would be even more worried if they knew that I had overheard their conversation with Sam's father, so I couldn't ask them if they had any more news about the pogrom.

I just kept banging out a Bartok melody. More missed notes. Mother finally roused herself.

"Nelly, please! You're not trying!"

"Yes I am!"

She sighed, then glanced at her watch. "Look at the time! You should be getting ready for your piano lesson."

I hurried to gather up my music books because my piano teacher became furious if I was ever late. Suddenly, the door to the room flew open and Father rushed in, still wearing his stethoscope. He was seething with excitement.

"Kati, listen! The American radio station, *The Voice of America*, just announced that the borders to Austria are still completely open. The Revolution has made everything chaotic, and no one is guarding the frontier. Thousands of people are fleeing the country. This is our chance. Imagine being free! We must act quickly. Who knows how long this situation will last. The Russians might seal off the borders any minute."

"Oh, Vili," Mother said quietly, "are you sure it's safe? Shouldn't we consider what to do a little longer? It's such a big step. To leave our home, our country . . ."

Father finally noticed me with my music satchel in hand. "Where are you going, Nelly?"

"I have a piano lesson in twenty minutes."

"You'd better phone Mrs. Lepke. Tell her you're sick. I don't want you out of the house just now. Where is Ida?"

"She's playing in our room."

"Look, Kati," he said, turning to Mother, "this is not a time for talk. We must seize this opportunity while we can. We may never get a chance like this again. I've heard that the Austrians are waiting with trucks on their side of the border to help the Hungarian refugees."

"If you're quite sure, Vili . . ."

Father held her shoulders tightly. "I am, Kati, I am. I have never been more sure of anything in my whole life. I have it all figured out." His voice was fast and steady. "We can drive down to Csorna; it's only three miles from the border. We'll say that I was called to treat the cattle on the collective farm just past the town, and you and the children came along to visit the Szabos. What do you think?"

Mother nodded reluctantly. "When do you want to leave?"

"What do you mean, leave?" I interrupted. "I'm not going anywhere! After my piano lesson I'm tutoring Sari in Russian, and then some of us are going over to her house to listen to records."

"Quiet, Nelly!" Father said impatiently. "I don't have time for your nonsense now." He turned to Mother. "Kati, the sooner we leave, the better. We don't know how much longer the borders will be open. Pack a small bag with only the absolute essentials. We should be gone within the next twenty minutes. And Kati," he added, "both you and the girls should act as if you're going on an outing to the country."

I've always loved traveling in Father's old black car, but this trip was different. None of us spoke. The silence was a passenger along with Ida, me, and our parents. We were all dressed in our best clothes. I was wearing a gray pleated skirt and a hand-knit red sweater with a pattern of yellow roses around the neck. My new green loden coat was very hot and I was afraid that it would become permanently wrinkled. I could hardly breathe. I felt like a sardine squashed between Mother and Ida in the back seat. But I refused to utter even a single word, for I had sworn never again to speak to Father as long as I lived. I had approached him before we left the house, while Mother was packing an overnight bag.

"Father," I pleaded, "you can't be serious about leaving. You can't expect me to go! I can't leave my friends. I really can't!"

Father was scowling, not really hearing me. "Quiet, Nelly! This doesn't concern you!" he said.

"What do you mean it doesn't concern me? I'm not going! You can't make me!"

"You'll do as you are told, young lady!" Father was getting red in the face.

"You can't make me!"

"You'll do as you are told!" Father repeated. "We're leaving in fifteen minutes."

I knew from past experience that it would be impossible to reason with Father once he became so angry, but at least I wanted to say good-bye to Sari and Miki. I picked up the phone to call them.

"What do you think you're doing?" Father cried, as he snatched the phone out of my hand and hung it up.

"I'm calling Sari to say good-bye."

Father took a deep breath, and even tried to smile.

"You can't call anyone, Nelly," he said. "It might put the whole family in danger if you tell anybody what we're planning. It's also safer for your friends not to know anything, in case something goes wrong."

I felt ill. "I just can't go without calling them, Father. Surely you must see that." I wished I could control the shaking in my voice.

Father's expression softened. "Nelly, I'm afraid we have no choice. Absolutely no phone calls. Your mother and I aren't saying good-bye to anyone, either."

I was quivering with anger. "You're a tyrant! I hate you!" I knew I shouldn't be talking to him so rudely, but I couldn't stop myself. "If you don't let me call Miki and Sari, I'll never talk to you again as long as I live!"

"Be reasonable, Nelly. You're not a little girl anymore."

I astonished myself by yelling at him. "I don't care! You're just being mean!"

"I don't have time to argue with you. Just do as you're told," Father said. And he turned his back on me and walked away. My heart pounded so hard I thought I could hear it throbbing.

Now Father was sitting in the passenger seat and Jeno, his assistant, was driving. They were much more comfortable in the front than the three sardines in the back. Ida hadn't heard us yelling, so she didn't suspect that anything unusual was taking place. She was fidgeting and squirming beside me in the car. I gazed past her out the window, but couldn't see anything interesting. There were only a few farmers working in the fiery autumn fields, grazing livestock, and the occasional horse-drawn buggy clopping by. A deep exhaustion had seeped into my bones. I sat yawning, as if I had been awake for days.

"When are we going to get there?" Ida asked for the millionth time.

"Be quiet!" I poked her with my elbow.

"Be nice to your sister," Mother said automatically.

"I'm so bored," Ida whined. "Let's sing." Whenever we took car trips, our whole family sang together.

"I've been working on the railroad," Ida trilled.

"Tra, la, la, tra, la," answered Mother, who could never remember the words to a song. I didn't join in.

"Come on, Nelly, sing," Ida said.

"Do they have to make so much noise?" Father interrupted.

"Oh, Vili! Leave them alone. They're just children. They don't understand what's going on."

"Of course I do! Don't treat me like a baby." I couldn't help speaking up.

"What's going on?" Ida asked.

"Nothing for you to worry about," Mother answered.

"I'm hot," Ida complained, "I want a drink."

"Later, dear, later."

"Remember, Jeno," Father said, "wait until the evening—seven or eight o'clock at the latest—and then go to the house and take anything you want—furniture, dishes, knickknacks, anything at all. And keep the car."

"I'll miss you, Dr. Adler." Jeno's voice cracked.

"Now don't get emotional, Jeno." Father was sounding very emotional himself. "Let's just hope everything goes smoothly."

"What's going on?" Ida whispered to me.

"Hush, Nelly," Mother said, preventing me from answering her.

"Only three more kilometers to go," Father said.

"Vili, look!" Mother cried, pointing to the road. A dozen Russian soldiers in khaki uniforms were blocking the road with two large trucks. It was impossible for us to pass without stopping.

"Oh my God! A roadblock!" Mother said in agonized tones.

"Girls, no matter what happens, whatever they ask you, don't answer any questions," Father said urgently. Ida began to cry as Jeno slowed down the car.

A burly soldier in a Russian army uniform approached us, pointing his rifle at Father's head. Black spots appeared before my eyes. I could hardly breathe.

"What's the matter, Sergeant?" Father asked, his strong voice masking his fear. I noticed that the whole group of chattering and laughing soldiers had guns strapped to their shoulders.

"Where . . . headed?" the sergeant asked in broken Hungarian. "You . . . papers?"

"Certainly, Officer. I have a travel permit. I'm a veterinarian." Father handed over his documents. The soldier finally lowered his gun. My heart stopped racing. "I'm going to innoculate some cattle on the collective farm near Csorna. This is my assistant," Father said, pointing to Jeno. "I was worried about leaving my wife and children alone, so I brought them along with me to visit some friends in Csorna while I'm at work."

The soldier seemed to understand what Father was saying. He ambled over to an older man leaning against the truck, who must have been the colonel. The old man's shiny, bald head reflected the sun's rays. To my horror, I felt laughter bubbling in my throat. The sergeant and the colonel were whispering to each other. I bit the inside of my cheek to stop my laughter from spilling out. They were speaking Russian so rapidly that I couldn't understand what they were saying. Both soldiers returned to the car and ordered us to get out. They searched the car thoroughly, looking in the trunk, under the seats, and even in the glove compartment. I found out later that Jeno had hidden the little money Father had saved and the gold bracelet Mother had inherited from her grandmother under the upholstery of the car on the driver's side. Fortunately, the soldiers didn't look there. My parents and Jeno seemed completely at ease. I followed suit by behaving as normally as possible. If only I didn't feel like laughing. Ida was still wailing at the top of her lungs.

"I . . . just . . . looking. . . ." the sergeant mumbled. He handed back Father's documents. "Everything . . . in order."

"Why is the little girl crying?" the colonel asked in a guttural but fluent Hungarian, pointing his gun at Ida. "What is she afraid of? Where are you going, little girl?" He kept the gun pointed at Ida and his eyes on Father while he was talking. I no longer felt hysteria. Father and Jeno stood completely still, and Mother began to quiver like an autumn leaf in the breeze.

I forced myself to speak up. "Ida is afraid of

her own shadow. She always cries when she sees anybody wearing a uniform." This time I forced myself to laugh. I had to clench my hands to stop their trembling.

The colonel's expression softened. "Here," he said, taking a package of mints from his pocket and handing a candy to both Ida and me, "this should make her feel better."

"Can we go on now?" Father asked. "I have a lot of work this afternoon."

The colonel hesitated for a moment. "I think that you should return to Veszprem, Comrade Adler. It's not safe to travel in the countryside nowadays, Comrade," he said with a false smile. I noticed he kept his hand near the handle of the revolver in the holster around his waist. "We'll accompany you back home, to make sure that you get there without any trouble. This is being done for your own protection, you understand," he added. He called to two of the young soldiers standing in front of the trucks, "Hey you, Sergei, and you, Ivan, you drive!"

I sensed my parents' and Jeno's terror now, although they weren't revealing it. I was frightened, but I knew instinctively that I couldn't show how I was feeling, no matter what happened. We must have presented a striking tableau—the small, black car flanked by the two huge, green army trucks with the gently rolling hills as a backdrop. The melancholy Russian ballads the soldiers were singing rang unnaturally loud in the sleeping hills. Inside the car none of us felt any desire to talk. Father spoke only once.

"Remember," he warned us, "no matter what you are asked, no matter what you are told, you will only answer that I was going to do some field work and you were coming along to visit the Szabos in Csorna."

"Yes, Father," I replied. Ida began to cry once again. You'd think she would have run out of tears by now. But no such luck!

As we entered Veszprem, Jeno signaled to turn in the direction of our house, but the old colonel, no longer silkily polite, brusquely ordered us to follow him. We finally rolled to a stop across the street from the Russian military headquarters. The bald soldier motioned with his gun for Father to follow him into the squat, gray building with the barred windows.

"I'll be only a few minutes, Kati," Father said reassuringly. "Wait here until I return."

We waited and waited, but Father didn't come back. Mother, her teeth chattering, was praying under her breath. It was a sunny afternoon, but the coming winter was chilling the air. The streets were full of people. Sam Gabor and his father walked by on the sidewalk. Sam recognized our car and turned toward us to say hello, but his father pulled him away before he could talk to me. Several others passed by with averted eyes while we sat in the car waiting. Not one of them stopped to chat or ask why we were there, across the street from the Russian headquarters.

Three hours passed. It was getting dark and cold. It had been hours since we had eaten some bread and butter in the car and I was ravenous. Just when I couldn't bear waiting any longer, Mother turned to me.

"I'm going to see what's going on," she whispered frantically. "Father should be back by now."

"I'll come with you," I told her.

"No, no! You stay here with Ida and Jeno. It's too dangerous," she said, getting out of the car.

I climbed out after her. "I'm coming with you. You can't stop me. If you leave me, I'll follow you. You need me to translate for you. They probably don't speak Hungarian."

"Oh, Nelly, you're stubborn like your father." Mother sighed in defeat. "All right, come along. They're not likely to hurt a child."

"I'll pretend that I'm sick, and we want Father to take us home. Maybe they'll let him go then."

Mother thought for a moment. "Not a bad plan," she admitted reluctantly.

We crossed the road and entered through the steel doors of the building. I doubled over and clutched my stomach, as if I were in pain. A young Russian soldier with blond hair and an older, darker one, were sitting at a desk by the door. They were both wearing revolvers. Two machine-guns were leaning against the wall behind the desk.

"Halt! Where do you think you're going?" the younger one barked in Russian.

"Tell them we want to see your father," Mother whispered, clutching my hand.

I opened my mouth to answer, but no sound came out. I licked my lips and croaked in Russian, "My father! I've got to see my father! I feel sick!" Five years of Russian classes in school were finally paying off. I began to sob and rub my eyes. It didn't take much effort to cry and whine. "I want my father! We want father!" I moaned and clutched my stomach.

The young soldier seemed sorry for me. "What's your father's name?"

"Dr. Vilmos Adler. He came in with a bald soldier a long time ago."

"Oh, you must mean Colonel Tolchinsky." He frowned, scratching his nose in an undecided manner.

"Tell him again that you're sick," Mother whispered under her breath.

"Oh, I feel so sick! I think I'm going to throw up!" I said to the soldier in Russian. And I began to cry again.

The soldier jumped back in alarm. "Don't you dare!" he thundered. "Come on, follow me!" He explained something in rapid Russian to the other soldier but I couldn't understand him. Then he led us through a gray maze lined with identical brown doors. He finally knocked on a door at the end of a hall.

"Come in!" I recognized the bald colonel's voice. He was standing by the door, revolver in hand. Father was slumped over a battered oak table. His face was a dull gray colour, his forehead beaded with sweat. The bright light shining into his face revealed a thin rivulet of blood running down the side of his head from a cut above his right eye. My knees were shaking, and I could feel the sweat trickle down my back.

"Are you out of your mind to bring them here?" the old colonel barked.

The young soldier shrank away from him. "They made such a fuss I didn't know what to do," he said sheepishly. Mother's face was ashen and she was leaning against the door, her hand covering her mouth.

"You shouldn't have come," Father whispered. He was speaking so quietly that I ran up to him before the guards could stop me and put my ear up to his lips to hear what he was saying.

I realized that I mustn't ask why he was bleeding. I remembered to clutch my stomach. I didn't have to pretend to cry anymore. "I am so sick, Father. Take me home! Mother isn't feeling well, either. Look how pale she is." I took hold of Father's hand and squeezed his fingers. He squeezed back. I saw approval in his eyes.

"Colonel, my daughter is very ill and my wife is extremely upset. Let me take them home. You know where to find me if you want to speak to me again." I was proud of the courage in Father's quiet voice.

The Russian hesitated. He seemed to be making up his mind. He glanced at me and his eyes softened for a moment. "Go," he said in his old gruff tone, "but don't leave town." The sigh of relief exploding from Father's lips filled the dusty silence. I pretended a coughing fit to cover it up.

"Enough! Go! Get out of here! But don't think that I am finished with you!"

Father was leaning on me heavily, barely able to walk and Mother was taking deep breaths, clutching my other arm. The walk to the front entrance took an eternity.

By the time we crossed the street, Mother had recovered. "Thank God you're alive! What did they do to you?" she asked Father.

"Later, later, Kati. . . . Let's go home."

Mother and I helped Father to the car. He was in pain. When we got home, we saw that his back was a patchwork of black and blue bruises and oozing cuts. He told us the Russian had whipped him with the muzzle of his gun. Mother called the doctor, who prescribed painkillers for him. We were just thankful that Father wouldn't have any permanent damage.

That night, Mother stole into our room while Ida slept and I pretended to. She unpacked our traveling bag and straightened our dresser drawers. I understood that this was to ensure that everything seemed as if we had never left. My mind was teeming with all the stories I had heard about the dreaded secret police, the AVO, searching people's homes in the middle of the night. What if they decided to pay us a call? Did they want Father? Did they take away children? I tossed and turned for hours before falling asleep.

5

Escape

I am all alone and running, running with all my might. Suddenly, I stumble and fall. It takes me a moment to realize that the noise piercing the eerie darkness is my own labored breathing. Now I am on my hands and knees, crawling in the dirt, trying to get my bearings. My groping fingers find a large, rectangular object, smooth and cold to the touch. It's the headstone on my great-grandfather's grave! The marble is cracked in two, and the flowers around it are trampled, dead, except for one perfect white rose. I bend down to smell the flower. My fingers caress the petals. They feel silken in my hand. A thorn pricks my finger and blood begins to ooze from beneath my fingernails, but I feel no pain. A sickening smell assaults my nose. I know it to be the stench of burning flesh, although I have never smelled it before. Suddenly, the thundering sound of horses' hooves tears through the cocoon of stillness that was engulfing the cemetery. I can hear them coming closer, closer. At first, only the faint outline of an army is visible in the darkness. As it approaches, I can see a flag with a swastika flapping in the wind. A lone moonbeam escapes the clouds' embrace and reveals the face of the flag bearer astride an enormous black horse. I try to scream, but no sound escapes my throat. I behold in mute horror a hyena face with its mouth gaping open in silent laughter. Looking down, I see a furry paw clutching the flag. A great flash of lightning assaults the inky sky, the stallion rears on its mighty legs, and suddenly it is a malevolently grinning Colonel Tolchinsky who is riding the horse and grasping the flag, which is now decorated with a hammer and sickle. I know that I have to escape, to keep running, but I cannot move. I strain to get up, but I am rooted to the grave. I have become the gravestone.

My heart was pounding so rapidly when I awoke that I could hardly breathe. My pyjamas were drenched with sweat. I longed to run to Mother and Father to tell them about my nightmare, but I knew I couldn't. They deserved happy and well-adjusted children. So, instead, I just peeled off my wet pyjamas and stuffed them into the clothes hamper. Anyway, my parents were too preoccupied today to pay much attention to me. Father was moving about very carefully, as if he were trying to skirt the pain. Mother was hovering about, irritating him with her anxiety. She was so cheerful that she almost convinced me of her good mood until I noticed the little muscle twitching uncontrollably by her mouth.

A few hours later, we were sitting around the dining-room table. Lunch was always a hot meal in our house. Today, it was sauerkraut cabbage and noodles. Father was pensive.

"Thank God, this whole escape business is finished," he said. "I want you girls to forget what happened yesterday. Nothing in the world would get me to repeat the experience. You know, I'm almost glad we got caught. We acted too hastily, without thinking things through."

"You're right, dear." Mother nodded her head in agreement. "I always felt that the whole situation was too risky. Let's put the entire ordeal behind us and carry on with our lives as usual."

I felt relieved. "Does this mean we won't have to leave our friends?" I wanted to be sure.

"Hush, Nelly," Mother said. "As your father said, forget yesterday. Never mention it again."

She didn't have to worry. I was too scared to talk about what had happened. I couldn't forget the secret police. I kept repeating to myself all the stories I had heard about the AVO, and how they took away innocent people in the middle of the night. I thought about Rozsi not knowing where her father was. Nothing could be worse.

I was so exhausted from fright that I couldn't even think clearly. I tried to push all thoughts of the Russians out of my mind and concentrated on hiding a huge yawn behind my hand. "What are we going to do after lunch? I wish school would start again," I said to Mother.

"Stop yawning, Nelly! It's a rude habit!" Mother responded automatically. "Why don't you practice for an extra half hour? That'll give you something to do. And don't forget, Mrs. Lepke wants you to go for your piano lesson at two o'clock to make up for the one you missed yesterday." I was sorry that I had ever spoken. "And, Ida," Mother continued, "there is no need for you to be lazy, either. This afternoon, we'll review your multiplication tables and work on your penmanship. Then you'll be ahead of the other students when school reopens."

Ida groaned. She hated arithmetic almost as much as I hated the piano. The doorbell rang.

"I'll get it!" I said, glad to have an excuse to leave the table.

"Stop!" Father said. He exchanged frightened looks with Mother. Painfully, he rose and shuffled like an old man to the door. The minutes passed with excruciating slowness before he showed Dr. Gabor into the room. Dr. Gabor was flushed with excitement.

"Hello Kati, children. Vili told me what happened to you yesterday. It's unfortunate that you had to go through all that, but it was simply a case of bad luck. You should never have tried going by car. The borders to Austria are still open. The railway workers are running a train to Csorna in spite of the national general strike. Vili, we will be on that train. Most of the other Jews in our city will be on it, too."

Father and Mother gazed at each other silently. Father let out a great sigh. "Nelly, Ida," he said, "eat your lunch while Mother and I listen to what Erno has to say. Who knows, we may still have a chance to become free."

56

I felt sick to my stomach. What was wrong with them? Didn't they learn anything yesterday?

An hour later, I was hurrying toward the railway station by Jeno's side, Ida clutching my hand. My parents had felt it would be safer for us to split up. Jeno walked so fast that I had trouble keeping up with him, and Ida kept tripping on the rough sidewalk. We saw a few familiar faces along the way, but Jeno dragged me away before I could even say hello.

"Hurry," Jeno whispered urgently, "your parents are waiting. I don't want to be late. They'll worry." We were to meet Mother and Father at the train station.

In Jeno's pocket was a large wad of folded paper money. I had watched Father slip it into his hand before we left.

"I'd like your promise, Jeno," Father had said, "that if anything happens to Kati or me, you'll take care of the girls until we're released."

"You don't even have to ask me, Dr. Adler. I look upon the children as my own. But nothing will happen to you. Everything will be fine. You'll see."

"I certainly hope so, Jeno. But I must think of the children first. A second capture would be disastrous."

It was difficult to think clearly at the speed Jeno was rushing us along. By the time we got to the station I was out of breath. As soon as we arrived, I saw my parents standing at the station entrance. Father had his arm around Mother and they were anxiously scanning the busy throng of people. They greeted us with hugs and kisses. I was surprised at their appearance. Even though new clothes were very expensive and hard to find in

Hungary, Mother was so clever with her needle that she was always fashionably dressed. She could make any hand-me-down look brand-new. But not today. She was wearing a ratty brown coat I'd never seen before, and her gardening shoes with mud-coated heels. Father, too, was unusually shabby in a cracked leather coat he wore to work when he had to examine animals in the barns. A small overnight bag in Mother's hand was our sole luggage. Father wanted to ensure that the Russians wouldn't be suspicious if they stopped us again. Mother had also dressed us to look shabby. Ida and I were wearing our old school jackets. Mine was far too short in the sleeves.

My beautiful velvet dress hung in a cupboard at home—in a room I might never see again. Our room was full of our possessions; our school books were still there, as if they were waiting for us to take them up again. I thought of my beautiful shells sitting on my bookshelf in the room forever empty of us.

It was hard to say good-bye to Jeno. Mother shook his hand warmly and Father embraced him. I blinked back my tears and gave him a quick hug and Ida kissed him. Looking back one last time, we elbowed our way into the overcrowded railway car, and were immediately swallowed up by the strangely excited crowd. There were so many travelers that while Mother and Ida found seats on the scarred, wooden benches in another coach, Father and I had to stand for the entire hour-and-a-half-long journey. Every time the old railway car banged and rattled I knocked into Father, until he put his arm around my shoulder to steady me. I pressed my face into his jacket, and the familiar smell of cows and horses comforted me. Father was lost in thought and barely spoke to me. I amused myself instead by thinking of ways to see Miki next weekend without Mother finding out. Suddenly, I realized that I might never see Miki again. Or Sari. Could a person's heart actually break from sadness? This was the worst moment. Not to see Miki, not to be with Sari. Would they miss me? Would they understand that I didn't say good-bye because Father wouldn't let me? I wanted to kick and bawl like a baby, but I knew I couldn't let my parents down.

I had always been proud of Father because everybody in our district knew and respected him. Now he struck up a conversation with the men standing next to us. "Well, Mr. Kovacs, where are you off to?" he questioned a plumber from our town. Mr. Kovacs fixed our toilet once when Ida flushed her doll instead of fishing it out when it fell into the bowl.

Mr. Kovacs winked at us. "The same place as you, doc," came his quick reply. "The same place as everyone else on this train." And all the people around us began to laugh. Even Father's chest rumbled against my face.

I had only been on a train once before, when Jeno took me to visit his parents in the small village where he was born. Ida was too little to come. Jeno and I ate a picnic lunch of kolbasz, with a piece of heavy dark rye bread, and green peppers. I loved that.

The railway car was rattling and swaying and it made me feel queasy. As the train crossed a small bridge, I felt my heart lurch at the sight of a group of lounging Russian soldiers with their guns beside them on the ground. Even thinking of the Russians made me temble.

I was also so hot that I felt I couldn't draw enough air into my lungs. Before leaving the house, I had put on my heavy blue cardigan sweater and my red pullover, and stuffed my pockets with three pairs of woollen mitts. I even pulled three more pairs onto my hands—the fuzzy purple ones I wore for tobogganing, the blue mitts with a reindeer pattern, and the new red pair Ida had knitted for my birthday. My hands always got cold easily, and I had thought that wherever we were going, extra mittens would be useful. But now my fingers were prickling with the heat, and sweat was trickling down my back. I reached into my pocket. The extra mittens were still there. So was my lucky rabbit's foot. It was very powerful. I was hoping that if it could help me get good marks in school, it might protect us while we were trying to escape. I gave it three strokes for good luck.

We arrived in Csorna at three o'clock in the afternoon. It would be dark soon, and the wind was whipping the last of the leaves along the platform. My parents were delighted to see their friends the Brauns at the station. The Gabors with their son, Sam, were getting out of another coach.

"We were hoping to meet other arrivals from Veszprem," Mr. Braun said. "We wanted to let you know that our townspeople are gathering in the schoolyard on Rakosi Avenue."

"We should get off the streets immediately or the police will pick us up," Father said.

"You're quite right," said Dr. Gabor. "Let's set out for the schoolyard immediately. We can wait there until nightfall, when it'll be safer to cross the border."

It took just a few minutes to reach the elementary school. My parents were busy talking to their friends, and Ida to Adam Braun, who was a nice boy. That left me with Sam. "Oh, Nelly, it's you. I thought it was an elephant," he said clasping his arms together in front of him like a trunk. I turned away in my many layers of clothing. "Nelly is a snob! Nelly is a snob!" he jeered.

I was relieved to see some of my friends in the dusty schoolyard. I recognized at least a dozen families from Veszprem among the hundreds of people crowded into the small playground. The schoolyard, separated from the surrounding fields with a chain-link fence, was seething with activity. Clusters of people were earnestly talking, smoking and planning their futures. Some of the men were sprawled on the cold ground, while the women were perched on suitcases. The older children congregated by the fence and the little ones, like Ida, were drawing hopscotch squares in the dust or playing tag. Father seemed elated, chatting and joking with his cronies. But, as time passed, his energy drained away. I watched him call Mother away from a group of women. He put his arm around her shoulders. They were so absorbed in each other that they didn't notice I was standing close enough to overhear them.

"Kati," Father said, "are we doing the right thing? I'm not so certain anymore. This is much harder than I thought. It's not easy to leave home. You know, it's still not too late for us to go back."

"I'm not sure, Vili. I just don't know. . . ." It was not like Mother to be so hesitant. "We've got lots of time," she continued. "It's only four o'clock. Let's visit the Szabos. They may have heard some news from Austria. Maybe Imre can advise us what to do."

I was pleased to hear this. Mrs. Szabo claimed that Ida and I were her adopted grandchildren, and she always served us delicious home-baked cookies. It was a few minutes walk to the Szabos' red-brick house, but it seemed completely deserted. No one answered the doorbell.

"Let's try once again," Father said. I banged so hard that my knuckles were sore.

We were about to leave when Mother noticed a corner of the lace curtain flutter in the parlor window. A moment later the front door opened a crack, and small, wizened Mrs. Szabo stuck her head out. She motioned for us to come in.

"Kati, Vili, and the children too. How nice to see you! But you should have phoned first. Imre is out on a call," she said in a fluttery voice.

"That's okay, Emma, don't worry about that," Father told her. "We're leaving Hungary. We're planning to cross over to Austria tonight. Have you heard if it's safe?"

The old lady exhaled a deep sigh of relief. "Come on," she said, as she opened the parlor door, "I want you to meet Edit, my sister, and her husband, Bela." She pointed to a middle-aged couple sitting on the couch. "They have the same plans as you do. Unfortunately, Imre and I are too old to join you. Coffee, anyone?"

"I am not allowed to drink coffee, but I'd love to have a cookie," Ida volunteered. Everybody laughed.

After our visit with Mrs. Szabo, my parents seemed to be more sure of their decision. The sun had almost set by the time we reached a collective farm five kilometers from Csorna. We had walked for an hour and a half and we were exhausted. The Brauns and the Gabors walked with us. Father's practice used to bring him to this area and he knew the countryside well. Although it was quite dark, I could see the shadowy outlines of thirty or so thatched-roof farmhouses surrounded by huge barns and fields. An old farmer, with skin almost as brown as the fertile earth he tilled, greeted us politely at his door and introduced himself as Janos Kicsi. Ida snorted when she noticed that he had a habit of twirling his luxurious mustache as he spoke.

"Friends in Csorna told us you might be able to guide us to the Austrian border, Mr. Kicsi," Father said.

The old man sized us up thoughtfully, spat on the ground, and finally replied, "Without any difficulty, sir. But there is still too much daylight. We'll have to wait about half an hour until it's completely dark, and then I can take you and your friends to a spot where you can cross safely into Austria." I watched as, for the second time today, Father slipped someone a large wad of folded paper money.

We sat on a hard wooden bench in Kicsi's overheated kitchen waiting for darkness to fall. I shifted my weight and moved my feet to get comfortable, but with no success. I was so tired that I had to prop my eyes open with my fingers to keep from falling asleep, until Mother ordered me to stop. Ida was also squirming about. Kicsi was frying sausages on his wood stove. The delicious smell made my mouth water. Oh, how I wished he would give us some! But he cut himself a slice of dark bread and polished off the entire portion by himself.

There was nothing to do but think. It suddenly hit me that I, Nelly Adler, age thirteen, was about to embark upon the most important journey of my life. Of course, I was scared. Only a fool would disregard the dangers in our situation. At the same time, I was gripped by a strange sense of anticipation. I felt like a heroine in one of the adventure stories I'd always loved to read. I told myself that this was how the great explorers of the past, like Christopher Columbus, must have felt before embarking upon voyages into the unknown. Did Phileas Fogg, the hero in Jules Verne's novel *Around the World in Eighty Days*, feel the excitement I was experiencing now? My eyes were getting heavier and heavier until I was startled into wakefulness by Kicsi suddenly pushing himself away from the rough-hewn kitchen table and announcing, "It is time now."

Father, deep in thought and fidgeting with the button on his coat, took a deep breath, squared his shoulders, and stood up. "Let's go, then."

"I'll bring the cart around to the gate," the farmer offered.

In a few moments, we heard his approach. Father climbed up beside Kicsi. The rest of us sat in the wagon of the horse-drawn buggy. Ida was between Mother and me, and we were all facing the Brauns. Sam, who was with his parents behind us, poked me with his feet. I pretended not to notice. The straw in the bottom of the cart tickled my chin, and made Ida sneeze. Kicsi was just pulling in the reins of the large brown horse and preparing to leave when a pale young man, flourishing a machine-gun, dashed out of a barn by the gate. He hopped onto the buggy and sat down beside Father.

"I'll come along to protect you good people," the young man declared in hearty tones that sounded false. I noticed that, although his lips were smiling, his eyes glistened like hard pebbles in the quickly falling darkness.

"Get away, Bandi! We don't want you along!" Kicsi shouted furiously and shook his fists at the intruder. The young man with the gun stood undecided under the farmer's fierce gaze. Finally, he shrugged his shoulders.

"Well, if that's what you want, go ahead without me," he muttered angrily. "But you'll regret it!" And he vanished as quickly as he had appeared. Kicsi unclenched his fists.

"Good riddance, I say! He is a two-faced traitor, that one. I wouldn't like to have him with us. He was the secretary of the collective farm and a fanatic Communist before the Revolution. Everybody hated him and was afraid of him. Now that he's unsure which side will win, he's trying to stay in favor with both the freedom fighters and the Communists. He'd sell his own mother for a profit, that one. We'd better get going before he comes back."

We were soon driving down a bumpy dirt road leading into a dark forest. It must have been in such a forest that Hansel and Gretel lost their way. The absolute silence of the night was broken only by the monotonous clopping of the horse's hooves, the whispering of the trees rustling in the wind, and the occasional hoot of a lonely owl. The moon and the stars were unable to escape the heavy embrace of the angry clouds. Had I been transported into a nightmare? Only Sam's ongoing commentary reminded me that this was reality and not a frightening dream.

"How much farther? When are we going to get there? Isn't this exciting?" he kept asking over and over again. I whispered for him to be quiet, but he continued. "Scaredy-cat, scaredy-cat! Are you scared?" he teased.

"I'm not the only one who's frightened," I replied, forgetting my resolution to ignore him. Under cover of the darkness, I turned and smacked him good and hard on the left shin. Mother noticed and reprimanded me in front of everyone.

The boundaries of the forest receded from view the deeper we penetrated into it. I would never have given Sam the satisfaction of admitting to being frightened by the darkness, but I was very glad when Ida snuggled up to me and slipped her hand into mine. We seemed to have been traveling forever, although it could not have been more than a half hour before Kicsi pulled in his reins and came to a full stop.

"There," he said, pointing into the darkness. "The Hungarian border is over there, about three hundred meters in front of us. As soon as you cross it you'll come to no man's land, the neutral territory between Hungary and Austria. The Austrian border is beyond that." I peered into the darkness but, no matter how hard I tried, I couldn't see a thing.

"I guess this is it," Father said, offering the farmer his hand. He was interrupted by a sudden, loud rustling noise coming from the adjacent woods. I was so startled that I jumped backward and accidentally knocked into Sam. He must have been afraid because he didn't even make fun of me. The noise was coming from the right side of the dirt road. It grew louder and louder. Finally, the bushes parted and a group of ten bedraggled but grinning Hungarian soldiers appeared in the clearing at the edge of the woods. They were all very young, and each one had a gun slung over his shoulder. The sight was too much for Ida, who started to bawl and hid behind Mother. The leader of the soldiers, a tall blond man, seemed overjoyed to see me.

"Nelly, is that really you?" he shouted as he approached with outstretched hands. "Don't you recognize me out of my soccer uniform?"

"Sanyi Toth! I don't believe it! Mother, Father, Ida! Do you remember Sanyi? He's been the top goalie of our soccer league for the past three seasons." My friends and I were great soccer fans and attended all the games of our local team. Ida often came with us. We knew all the players well. Many of them were only four or five years older than we were.

"Well, imagine meeting you under such circumstances, Nelly, Dr. Adler! We're here to guard the border but, as you can see, we're not exactly doing our job. We were just debating about crossing over to Austria ourselves. We didn't get paid this month because of the Revolution. We're hungry," Sanyi said, rubbing his stomach. "The farmers know we haven't got a penny, but they won't sell us anything to eat on credit." He looked at Father expectantly.

"Let me help," Father said. He reached into his pocket but came up empty-handed. "Oh, boys, I gave my last forint to the farmer who brought us here," he said in a panicky voice. The Brauns and the Gabors found themselves in the same situation.

"Well, that's too bad, doc," Sanyi said as he sat down on the ground. "That's really too bad." His tone had become much less friendly. "Sit down, boys," he told his friends, who joined him on the ground. "We haven't eaten anything since yesterday. We're too weak and tired to point out a good place to cross, a safe place without any mines."

"What are mines?" Ida asked.

"Bombs to blow you up," Sanyi said.

I looked at him contemptuously. "Don't worry, Ida. Everything will be fine." I took her hand in mine. She squeezed my hand so hard that my new birthday ring cut deep into my finger. It was then that the idea came to me. My new ring was made of gold, so it must be very valuable. Would the soldiers accept it instead of money? I didn't want to give it to them—it was the only thing left from my grandmother and I had sworn I'd never take it off my finger. But, if I didn't give the soldiers the ring, we wouldn't be able to get to Austria, and Mother and Father might be arrested for trying to escape again. It became clear to me that I had no choice. I tugged at the ring, but had to struggle before I could get it off. It wanted to stay on my finger. It was so beautiful, gleaming in the moonlight. I held it out to Sanyi before I could change my mind.

"Nelly, I won't allow this!" Father whispered earnestly.

"Put the ring back on your finger," Mother said.

But, even as they spoke, we all knew there was no other way.

"Would you take this ring instead of money? It's real gold. Maybe you could sell it and buy food. So, what do you think?" I asked Sanyi.

"I think you've got yourself a deal," Sanyi said, pocketing the ring. "The farmers will feed us if we trade it for food. Why, even thinking about food makes us feel stronger, doesn't it fellows?" he asked his cronies. They all struggled back to their feet. "Let us show you a strip of land free of mines." Relief flooded my parents' faces. Sanyi parted the bushes and we followed him into the forest. Father patted me on the head and Mother kissed my cheek.

"Good girl," she whispered.

My ring finger felt light, as if it might float away from my hand. A branch scraped my cheek and distracted me before I could disgrace myself by crying. The soldiers led us through the forest to another dirt road, about a hundred meters from the clearing. We were greeted there by an amazing sight. A long column of eerily silent people, extending as far as the eye could see in the darkness, was steadily crossing the dirt road into the barren fields beyond. Some carried suitcases, while others had knapsacks on their shoulders. Mothers were hushing small children riding upon their fathers' backs. Gray-haired grandparents were being supported by their stronger sons and daughters. I held on tightly to Mother's arm, while Ida clutched Father's hand. As I gazed up at the outline of a watchtower in the distance, I lost my footing on the uneven ground and fell and grazed my knee. I barely noticed the pain.

"I'm really scared," Ida whispered.

"So am I," I replied before Mother hushed us. I felt so strange, almost numb. I felt as if everything were happening to somebody else, as if I were standing outside of my body, a spectator to the events around me.

I don't know how much time had passed before we could make out the dark shapes of the Austrians awaiting the arrival of the thousands of Hungarian refugees streaming like ants across the border.

As we reached Austria, and crossed the border into freedom, I felt surrounded by the almost palpable collective joy of the crowd. We all kissed and hugged, laughing and crying simultaneously. I even found myself grabbing Sam's hand.

"Well, we made it! We really made it!" Mother exclaimed.

"We did, didn't we?" Father shouted. He embraced her exuberantly. Ida and I held hands and jumped up and down in excitement, whooping with delight.

Within minutes, we were sitting in a huge tractor-drawn trailer, ready to be taken to lodgings for the night by our Austrian hosts. I would always regret that in my excitement I forgot to look back to catch a last glimpse of my native land.

6

Refugee Camps

Within ten minutes, the lurching trailer jolted to a stop in front of a huge, white stucco school building. There were at least three hundred of us bizarre holiday-makers. We were herded into a large auditorium reeking of gym shoes and human sweat.

A smiling, gray-haired woman, wearing the armband of the International Red Cross, greeted us. She was carrying a tray with glasses half-filled with a dark, sparkly fluid and a bowl of strange yellow fruit, the likes of which I had never seen before.

"Oh, Mother, can I have a drink?" Ida asked. "I'm so thirsty." My throat was also dry.

Ida gulped down some of the drink, but screwed up her face in disgust. "Ugh! It tastes terrible! I don't like it at all! It's much too sweet."

The woman from the Red Cross laughed, and told us it was a drink called Coca-Cola. I liked to try everything at least once. "It can't be so horrible," I told Ida, and bravely took a sip. "It's not too bad. You just have to get used to the taste."

Next, before Mother could stop me, I bit into the yellow fruit. It was awful! I gagged and spit it out.

"Oh, Nelly!" Mother said, trying not to laugh. "You've got to peel a banana before you eat it." We'd heard of bananas and Coca-Cola, but neither had been available in Hungary since the war.

Sam Gabor snickered. I quickly glanced around the room to see if anybody else was laughing at me. Nobody seemed to have noticed because they were listening intently to the local officials welcoming us to Austria. It felt odd not understanding a word of what they were saying. The German words all sounded the same to me, and they blended together until they no longer sounded like distinct words but simply noise. My parents spoke a little German, so they were able to understand that we would all sleep in the school's attic above us. To get there, we had to climb a steep ladder. Ida climbed the ladder sandwiched between Mother and Father. I followed behind, holding the wooden steps of the ladder so tightly that red indentation marks formed on my palms and fingers. I forced myself to look up, not down at the distant wooden floor. When we finally reached the top we found ourselves in a grim, windowless room with dirty walls decorated with banners welcoming the refugees to Austria. Straw was spread on the gray concrete floor. I remembered the lace curtains and the cozy armchairs of the room I had left behind.

I couldn't see beds anywhere. "Where will we sleep?" I asked Mother. She pointed silently to the straw.

"I don't like this place," Ida said.

Mother was becoming upset. "Vili, I cannot, I will not, sleep on the floor. This place is unfit for humans. It's like a stable. Why, some bug or animal from the straw might crawl into our clothing, which will be completely ruined in any case."

"I know, I know. This is an awful place. But there is nothing we can do about it. We'll just have to make the best of a bad situation."

"No, we won't! This is all a terrible mistake. Let's go back. Let's go home. Nobody even knows that we left." For the first time there was panic in her voice.

"Don't be foolish, Kati. Of course they do. We met at least six people we knew on the way to the station. You can't keep something like this a secret. People aren't fools. If we go back it's prison, or worse, for us."

Ida was looking back and forth from Mother to Father. She seemed on the verge of tears once again. I couldn't blame her. I clenched my teeth to avoid doing something that would upset my parents even more.

"What's the matter now?" Father snarled at Ida.

"I haven't got a pillow." Ida gulped.

Mother and Father looked at each other and began to smile. "A pillow! She wants a pillow!" Mother threw her head back and laughed. "We have no beds, no money, no home, but the child is upset because she hasn't got a pillow." Ida and I soon joined in their laughter. I was

73

laughing so hard that I thought I might never stop. Tears ran down my face.

"You want a pillow, I'll give you a pillow," Father said. He ripped the Welcome Refugees banner off the wall, folded it into a neat rectangular shape, and laid it down on the straw. "Here is a pillow, custom-made. A double one at that, big enough for both you and Nelly."

We lay down on the straw in our clothes, and used our coats to cover us. A Red Cross lady walked up and down the rows of makeshift beds and distributed bread and butter, coffee for the adults, and milk for the children. Best of all, she gave us writing paper, envelopes, and stamps so that we could contact friends and relatives back home. I hoped Father would let me have some of the stationery to write to Miki and Sari.

After awhile, I forgot the tickling of the straw and became quite comfortable. Perhaps I should have been thinking of freedom, but it was thoughts of Miki and Sari that crowded my head. When would I see them again? When would I be in my comfortable room at home? Oh, I hoped someone would look after my rock and shell collections. I kept thinking about my beautiful velvet party dress that I would probably never wear again. Ida was already gently snoring and I could feel my eyes getting heavier. I could barely hear Mother whisper to Father, "Oh, Vili, what have we done?" The next thing I knew, it was morning.

Breakfast was a repetition of supper the night before. Ida and I didn't mind at all, because by now we were thoroughly enjoying ourselves. It was as if the air were purer, the colors more vivid. I felt daring, like a pioneer, after yesterday's adventures. Knowing that we were refugees made us feel brave and special and rather important. Both Ida and I roared with laughter as we removed the straw from each other's hair and clothes. Ida was even more ticklish than I was. It was a good thing both of us wore our hair in braids. Mine was so curly that it would have been impossible to untangle it. Mother laughed along with us, but Father was in a dark mood and kept hurrying us to get ready.

"We'll miss the bus to Klosterneuburg if you two don't behave."

"What's in Klosterneuburg?" Ida asked for what must have been the millionth time, with an impish grin on her face.

Father sighed in exasperation. "As I've already told you, over and over again, we'll have to spend a few weeks in an immigrant camp until we receive permission to go to Vienna. We'll be staying in the old barracks, which were vacated by the Russian army when it left Austria. And we'll have to decide there what to do next, where to go, in which country we want to live. But I'm warning you, judging by our surroundings here, don't expect too much in the way of comfort," he said with a tight look on his face. "We'll just have to put up with any inconveniences. They won't last forever."

The holiday feeling had vanished. Even with Father's warnings still ringing in my ears, I was dismayed when we reached the refugee camp at Klosterneuburg. The squat, gray barracks were uglier than anything I could have imagined. Our wing lacked even the most basic amenities, and the bathrooms were the worst of all. The toilet cubicles had grimy walls, no doors for privacy, and the toilets were mere holes in the ground. Mothers had to accompany younger children to prevent them from falling in. Fortunately, the adjacent washroom, with its huge metal basin into which drained two dozen water taps, was like a playground for the children. Every evening we gathered there for huge water fights.

We were among the lucky ones. We were put into a group of six families, including the Brauns and the Gabors. We were given a smallish room lit by a single, bare bulb. Light filtered in through a gritty window high up on the wall and was dully reflected on the concrete floor. If I squeezed my eyes together tightly, the trickle of light formed a pattern on the walls that reminded me of the shadows cast by the lace curtains on the windows of my room at home. A sooty, black woodburning stove in the corner not only kept us warm, but also allowed us to toast our morning ration of bread. We were all issued big burlap bags stuffed with straw to serve as mattresses, and rough army blankets. We were also given one towel each and a paper bag containing a bar of harsh soap, a comb, and a toothbrush. Everything around us was dull and gray. My sun-dappled room at home seemed a million miles away. The light had even gone out of Mother's and Father's faces. They looked much older, with pinched expressions and worried looks in their eyes.

That first evening in the camp, Mother stated firmly that we had to change into our pyjamas. "You will not sleep in your clothing. It isn't civilized." She was devastated to discover that in her haste to pack she had only brought along my pyjama bottoms and Ida's pyjama top.

"Children, I'm so sorry." She said, biting on her lower lip. "To forget something so basic . . ."

"It's not important, Kati," Father said, hugging her. "We'll buy new pyjamas as soon as we can. At least the straw is covered here."

"I like sleeping in my clothes. Ida can wear my bottoms and her own pyjama top."

"That's not fair! I want to sleep in my clothes, too!" Ida cried.

"You see, the girls don't mind. They're enjoying themselves," Father said.

Mrs. Gabor overheard us and lent me an extra pair of Sam's pyjamas. Mother gradually calmed down, but occasionally a worried look flickered in her eyes. She was determined not to lower our standards, even under these strange conditions. Every evening, after we went to bed, Mother washed our underwear in the big metal tub in the washroom. Her hands became red and rough-looking, with the skin over the knuckles breaking open and bleeding, but she never complained that they were sore.

7

Letter to Sari

Father gave me some of the paper from the Red Cross, so I could finally write a letter to Sari. He also lent me the fountain pen he always carried in his shirt pocket. My hands trembled in anticipation as I began my letter. At last, I would be able to explain to Sari why I had left Hungary without saying good-bye. My fingers could hardly keep up with all the news I wanted to share, all the thoughts that flowed from my pen. I finished the letter in record time and was soon licking the envelope flap closed, ready to be handed over to the Red Cross lady for mailing. This is what I had written.

November 20, 1956
8:00 P.M.

Dear Sari,

This must be the first letter you have ever received from a refugee! I'm certain that by now you must have heard that we escaped from Hungary. Father says it's safer for you not to know the details, so I won't say anything about it except to tell you that I was scared the entire time. Well, in any case, that part of our journey is over now and, as you can see by the postmark on this letter, we're in an immigrant camp at Klosterneuburg in Austria. We'll be staying here until we receive permission to go to Vienna. Once we're there, we'll have to decide which country we want to emigrate to. My parents can't seem to make up their minds where they want to go.

Sari, don't be angry that I left without saying good-bye. Believe me, it wasn't my idea to leave like that. I wanted to call both you and Miki, but Father wouldn't let me.

I hope you can read this letter. I have to write with very tiny letters to save paper. Father says that we have only a few sheets left of the stationery given to us by a Red Cross lady. Please tell Miki that I'll write him as soon as I can get my hands on more paper and stamps.

How is everything at home? I miss you—and Miki! (But don't tell him!) Has school started again? Who is sitting next to you in my old seat? Have you been told by your Young Pioneers group leader which farm you'll be assigned to in the spring? Are you looking forward to working on a farm?

I feel like I'm in a different world here. Nothing is familiar. It's not that it's so terrible, but it's not home. And I don't feel like myself. I mean, I know I'm still the same person. I look the same, just a little less fat. But in other ways I feel so different. It's as if I am two people—one is the Nelly you know who went to school, talked to you in her room every day, and had a terrific birthday dance. The other Nelly, the immigrant Nelly, spends her days in the grimy barracks waiting for something to happen. This Nelly doesn't feel as if her life is happening to her. She feels like an onlooker, watching things happen to a stranger. This Nelly doesn't belong anywhere. There's nothing here—no school, no home. I even miss piano practice. I keep thinking about my nice things at home—my cozy room, my new party dress, and the gold ring I had to give away while we were escaping. I've also been worrying about my rock and shell collections. I want you to have them. And Miki should take my Jules Verne books. You know how much he loves adventure stories. Jeno has a key to our house. Ask him to let you in.

I'm never alone, not for a minute. Five families from Veszprem share a room with us. And—just my luck—one of them is the Gabors, Sam included. Eva Klein and her parents have the far corner. Remember how she danced at my birthday party? Ida is luckier than me. She has Eva's sister, Amy, to play with. You know, that little red-headed girl everybody calls Sis. She also plays with Adam Braun. None of us really likes Sam.

Mother and Father and the adults spend most of the day lying on the straw mattresses we use as beds, talking about the future and trying to decide which country to emigrate to. This has advantages for us. Ida and I, Eva, Sam, and the others run wild. As long as we keep out of their way, our parents let us do as we like. The huge barracks with its endless corridors is a wonderful place for races and hide-and-seek for the younger children, but I really miss my books. Eva has a paperback version of *Toldi*. That's the old epic poem about a famous Hungarian warrior that we'll be studying next year in school. Oh, I just realized what I wrote. I mean, that's what you'll be studying next year in school. I wish I would be sitting in the desk next to yours. Eva wants to be a movie star in America, so she always wants to take turns with me reading aloud from the poem. You should hear her! She pronounces every word in a loud dramatic voice. We act out the actions of all the characters. Both of us know most of the poem by heart now, which is lucky because the binding of the book broke yesterday and the pages are starting to fall apart. There are no other boys Sam's age in the camp. He looks so lonely that Eva and I usually let him join us out of pity.

Our room is so small that most of the floor space is taken up by the straw mattresses. We've got to step over at least half a dozen parents whenever any of us wants to go to the iron stove in the corner of the room to warm our hands or toast the bread we are given for breakfast. Every time any of us accidentally kicks or touches an adult on the floor, the victim complains bitterly. So, to avoid trouble, we stay out of the crowded little room as much as possible. But yesterday afternoon we finally ran out of ideas to keep busy. I actually found myself missing school until Sam made an announcement.

"I've got a fantastic plan, but you must all swear never to reveal it to anyone, or we'll get into a lot of trouble," he told us. We all clasped hands and swore on our grandmothers' graves never to betray his secret. (You know, like you and I used to.)

"What's this about, Sam?" Ida asked.

"Well, I've thought of a great new game."

I should have known better than to expect him to come up with something original. "A game! Who cares about a game? We're not babies who play games. I don't even want to hear your stupid idea." He makes me say vicious things even when I don't mean them.

"Be a good sport for once, Nelly," Sam said to me. Suddenly I was ashamed of myself because, to be fair, Sam has been bearable the last few days.

"Oh, okay. What are the rules of your stupid game?"

"Well, it's kind of like the Olympics. It tests your athletic abilities and how steady you are on your feet. We can all play it, even the younger ones." We all gathered around to hear his great plan. "This is what you've got to do. We all have to hop on one leg over our parents lying on the mattresses. The winner will be the first person to reach the stove without having kicked anybody," he explained.

"But won't our parents be mad at us if we bother them?" Sis asked.

"They'll kill us," I said.

"Not if they don't realize what we're doing," Eva told her sister with a twinkle in her eye. "Why, we could call ourselves the Veszprem Olympic Team, VOT for short." Eva loves acronyms.

We practiced in the hall for a few minutes, and then the VOT members crowded into the narrow doorway leading into our room. The adults had taken up their usual positions on the floor. Sam whispered under his breath, "On your mark, get set, go!"

Ida and Adam bumped into Mother on their second hop. Sis's foot grazed Mr. Braun's arm. I reached the stove first, with Sam and Eva in hot pursuit, until Eva tripped over her own mother. I couldn't believe it. Eva has been taking ballet lessons for five years. How could she be so clumsy!

"What's going on?" Dr. Gabor roared. "Have you all lost your minds? What are you children up to?"

"We were hungry and wanted something to eat," Eva said quickly, pointing to the leftover stew simmering on the stove.

"I wasn't born yesterday!" Dr. Gabor yelled. "What's going on here?"

Mrs. Klein quickly sat up on her mattress. "Are you accusing my child of lying?" she asked stiffly.

"Come, come," Mother said, "this is silly. Of course the children are hungry. Not surprisingly, for they hardly ate from this . . . slop at supper time. I'm glad they're finally ready to eat something." Then she took several of the tin bowls piled up on the rickety wooden table beside the stove, and ladled a huge portion of the abominable stew that's served for lunch and supper most evenings into each of the dishes. I could hardly force it down my throat. It was bad enough to have had to eat it the first time.

I had a stomach-ache the rest of the day. I was sure it was from the stew. Mother kept giving me questioning looks as I got ready for bed. I couldn't meet her eyes, no matter how hard I tried. Finally, I couldn't stand it anymore.

"Mother, I've got to tell you something, even though I swore not to, but . . ."

"No need to break your word, Nelly," Mother said gently, making me feel even worse. "I realized immediately what you were up to. As Dr. Gabor said, I wasn't born yesterday, either. But I think that you were punished enough by having to eat a second helping of the stew, don't you?" Wasn't it nice of her not to fuss over what we did?

Well, Sari, I've got to finish this letter now because I can hear Mother calling me to go to bed. I'll send you my address as soon as I have one.

Love,
Your friend forever,
Nelly

8

Ida's Birthday Party

Mother was asleep on the floor beside me, Ida was lying on one of the burlap mattresses on my other side, and Father was quietly snoring beside Ida. I had always been jealous of Ida's ability to fall asleep almost as soon as her head hit the pillow.

Suddenly, I was aware of a noise, but it took me a moment to identify the sound. Even though Ida was holding a pillow over her face, it didn't completely muffle her sobs.

"What's the matter?" She didn't answer, so I pulled the pillow away. "Come on, tell me what's bothering you."

"Oh, Nelly," she said between sobs, "everybody forgot that it's my birthday tomorrow. I want to go home."

"Don't be silly. We can't go home. We'd be put in jail if we did."

"No we wouldn't," she said hiccuping, with tears streaming down her face. "I don't like it here."

"Why didn't you remind Mother that it's your birthday?"

"I tried, but she never listens to me anymore. Mother doesn't love me anymore. I want to go home."

Poor Ida! At home she had always been cheerful and full of life. Lately, all she did was cry. I missed the little sister I used to have. I had to make her feel better somehow.

"Listen to me carefully. I'm going to tell you something I shouldn't. Mother would kill me if she found out that I told you, but we've been planning a surprise party for you for tomorrow." I didn't seem to have any control over the words that were coming out of my mouth.

"Oh, Nelly, really?" Now Ida was laughing and crying at the same time.

"I wouldn't joke about something so important. Mother's been talking to me about your party ever since we got here. Can you possibly imagine that she'd forget about your birthday? You'd better act surprised tomorrow, that's all I can say!"

"A real party, Nelly?"

"You'll see! Now don't ask me any more questions, or it won't be a surprise at all!"

It took a long time for Ida to calm down and fall asleep. I was very tired, but I sat up to keep awake because some serious thinking was in order. I was disgusted with myself. How could I have forgotten about

Ida's ninth birthday? She'd spent weeks knitting the red mittens for my party. And how could my parents forget? Didn't they care about us anymore? Even if we were refugees, shouldn't we still celebrate birthdays? But, as always, I felt guilty as soon as I had critical thoughts about my parents. Weren't they under a lot of pressure? Surely, they were different from their usual selves because they were so busy thinking about our new lives. I knew in my heart they still loved us. I felt the anger draining away. I had to tell Mother that we were giving a surprise birthday party for Ida tomorrow. When I was sure that Ida was fast asleep, I gently shook Mother's shoulders to waken her.

"What's wrong, Nelly?" She asked, startled. "Is something wrong?"

"No, but I've got to talk to you. You forgot that it's Ida's birthday tomorrow."

Mother was absolutely still for a moment. I couldn't see her expression in the darkness, but I could make out that she was covering her face with both of her hands. She didn't utter a single word for the longest time.

"Are you okay? Say something!"

"Yes, yes," Mother whispered. "I can't bear it that I forgot one of your birthdays." And she began to cry softly.

I felt like a monster. "Don't cry, Mother. It doesn't matter. Ida isn't upset anymore. She calmed down when I told her that we were planning a surprise party for her."

"Of course my forgetting about poor Ida's birthday matters, Nelly. Of course it does. I'm so glad you reminded me. Can you organize the entertainment? I think I can get us some sausages to roast in the stove. I'm afraid we won't be able to have a cake, but I'm sure Ida will understand."

As far as I was concerned, a birthday party without a cake was not a party at all. In Hungary, even when supplies were the hardest to obtain, Mother had scraped and saved until she was able to bake a birthday cake for each of our birthdays.

I woke up early and, by seven o'clock, I was already on my way to speak to Heinz, the head cook at the camp. Heinz, unfortunately, was my only hope. I knew my chances of getting him to bake a cake for me were very poor, but I felt I had to try. I could see a light filtering out below the kitchen door. Heinz would already have been at work for hours. He said that there weren't enough hours in the day to cook for the five thousand refugees housed in the barracks at one time. In addition, meals also had to be prepared for the large staff at the camp. I guess he was so nasty most of the time because he was too busy. I just hoped that he would be in a good mood today! Miracles sometimes did happen.

I knocked on the kitchen door, but there was no answer. I knocked again, harder this time. Still no answer. I banged on the door, but still no response. Somebody should have been there. The light was on. I pushed the door open gently. There was no sign of Heinz, but sitting in the center of the kitchen table was the most gorgeous cake I had ever seen—tall and round, with chocolate icing. Heinz must have been making some sort of special meal for the camp officials.

Ida loved chocolate cake. She wouldn't cry anymore if somebody baked a cake like this for her. I quickly glanced around the kitchen. There was no sign of Heinz. He must have gone to the washroom. My hands seemed to have a will of their own. They reached out and picked up the plate with the cake on it. I would tell Mother that Heinz had baked an extra cake and didn't need this one. As for Heinz, he'd never guess in a million years who had taken his cake. He didn't even let us children play in the corridor in front of his kitchen. I quickly peeked into the hall to make sure that nobody was there then, balancing the cake in front of me, I hurried back to our room.

Ida was amazed at the sight of her birthday cake. "It's the most beautiful cake I have ever seen. And mean old Heinz baked it for me!"

"I guess he isn't as bad as we thought," I told her. "We must have misjudged him. But now, let's get your party organized."

Ida wanted to have a dance, just like the one I'd had for my birthday. We pulled the burlap mattresses to the walls and turned on the radio, which Mother had borrowed from the camp's administrative office. Sam and Adam refused to dance with us, no matter how much we begged them. Ida was disappointed. It was hard to have a real dance without boys.

"Wait a minute," I told her. I pulled on my pyjama bottoms, and covered my long hair with Father's beret. Eva soon followed my example, but there was still something missing. We just looked like girls wearing pants until I happened to notice that Father was about to light the stove in the corner.

"Just a second!" I stopped him from lighting the fire just long enough to dip my fingers into the cold, sooty grate. With my blackened finger, I drew myself a large, curvy mustache above my upper lip. Eva followed suit and gave herself a beard. "Now we don't need the boys," I told Ida. "Eva and I can be the boys, and you and Sis can be the girls."

We took turns dancing with each other to the crackly radio music. When Sam and Adam saw how much fun we were having, they begged to join us.

"We're going to have a birthday picnic for Ida," Mother announced. She helped us rearrange the mattresses in a circle, and everybody sat down on the floor to eat the sausages and bread Father had toasted over the fire in the stove. We sang "Happy Birthday" to Ida and ate the beautiful cake. Ida said it was the most delicious cake she had ever eaten, but it tasted like sand in my mouth. When would Heinz notice that it was missing from the kitchen?

"We'll have to save Heinz a slice," Mother said. "It was extremely kind of him to give you the cake."

"Oh no, Mother. Heinz wouldn't eat cake. He is on a diet, trying to slim down." Before I could go on, Ida interrupted us.

"I'm having so much fun! This party is even nicer than Nelly's."

"Even though you haven't had any gifts yet?" Mother teased.

"I don't expect anything this year. I know we can't spend our money on gifts," Ida said.

"I'm very proud of you for being so understanding,

Ida. But what's a birthday without a nice gift?" Mother asked. With that, she took off her wristwatch and handed it to Ida. "It's time you had a grown-up watch, dear. Happy birthday. Be healthy and happy," she said, kissing her.

"You can't give away your watch, Mother," I said.

"I can't take it, Mother," Ida said, although I could tell by the way she was looking at it that she really wanted to keep it.

"Oh no, Ida. It's yours. And when I need a watch, you'll lend it to me, won't you? In any case, Father promised to buy me a new one, didn't you, Vili?" Father didn't reply, he just kissed her on the cheek. He had sold his own watch to get us money for necessities.

I felt terrible. I had nothing to give to Ida. Suddenly, I remembered the lucky rabbit's foot in my coat pocket. Ida was always asking to hold it, but I would only give it to her on special occasions. I took out the rabbit's foot, gave it a farewell squeeze, and handed it over.

"Here, Ida, this is for you. I'm too old for a rabbit's foot. I don't need it anymore."

Ida clapped her hands in delight. "Your rabbit's foot! Are you sure you want me to have it?"

"Of course I'm sure." I hugged her. I wished I could have held her forever. It felt so good to have the old Ida back again.

"I'll take good care of it," Ida promised, "and of your watch, Mother. These are the best gifts I've ever got. You really had me fooled for a while. I thought that all of you had forgotten my birthday."

It was past midnight when she finally fell asleep, still

wearing her watch and clutching the rabbit's foot in her hand.

Mother was very pleased with me. "You're a good sister, Nelly," she said, as she was getting ready for bed. "You made your sister very happy today. First thing tomorrow morning, I want you to come with me to thank Heinz for his generosity. Good night." And she was asleep almost immediately.

I tossed and turned the whole night. What would happen when Mother found out that I had stolen the cake? My parents would be so ashamed of me, and Heinz would be furious. What would Eva and Sam think? I should have thought of this before taking the cake. But Heinz would never have baked anything for Ida. And the cake had made her so happy.

The next morning, Mother was horrified by how exhausted I looked. She kept asking me if I felt sick. "Oh, I've just got a headache and a sore throat," I told her. "I guess I'm too sick to speak to Heinz."

"You most certainly are. I'll have to go by myself," Mother said.

"On second thought, I'd better come with you. After all, he gave the cake to me. I don't want him to think I don't have good manners."

On the way to the kitchen, I prayed and prayed for Heinz to be gone. But there he was, bent over the stove, stirring stew as usual.

"I'm Frau Adler," Mother said, "Nelly and Ida's mama. I want to thank you for giving Nelly such a beautiful cake yesterday. It made Ida so happy. The children have little enough happiness nowadays." She extended her hand to Heinz. Heinz held her hand for a long moment with a puzzled expression on his face until he noticed me standing behind Mother, my finger over my lips, desperately signaling him not to betray me. He didn't move a muscle.

"You're welcome, Frau Adler," the cook finally said. "I was happy to be able to help. Nelly is my favorite among all the children. I'm so glad you came to speak to me today, for I was going to look for you later myself. Yesterday, when Nelly asked me for the cake, she offered to help out in my kitchen. I told her I needed a dishwasher but, of course, only if you give your permission." He smiled at Mother innocently.

Mother was surprised. "Are you sure you want to do this, Nelly? You've never mentioned it before."

"Because I didn't think you'd let me. Heinz promised he'd teach me how to bake." I was amazed at my newfound talent for lying, and I was careful not to look at the cook.

For the next two weeks, I was Heinz's unpaid dishwasher. I hated putting my hands in the hot, greasy water, but I couldn't even complain about it or Mother would have made me stop, and then Heinz could have betrayed me. To give Heinz credit, he never mentioned the cake to me. He even gave me some of the brown wrapping paper in his kitchen as a farewell gift. I divided the paper into letter-sized sheets, so I would be able to write to Miki and Sari. I never told my parents what I had done, but I swore to myself I would never steal again. Not even for a good cause.

9

Letter to Eva

Three weeks after our arrival in Klosterneuberg a delegation of the Jewish relief agency, the HIAS, visited the immigrant camp and provided us with documents allowing us to leave the barracks. They even gave us train tickets. The Gabors obtained their papers and tickets at the same time as we did. One day later, I was traveling on an overcrowded train headed for Vienna with Sam sitting right behind me, peering over my shoulder to see what I was writing. I turned away from him, so he couldn't see a thing.

I was happy to leave the camp, but I also felt sadness at having to part from Eva. Her family had not yet received permission to leave Klosterneuburg. We had said our teary good-byes to each other this morning, vowing to remain friends forever. We also planned to write to each other often, keeping each other informed of our new lives. Why did I always have to leave my friends? First, I lost Sari and Miki, and now Eva. I felt so alone. A tear rolled down my cheek, and I bit my lip to keep from crying. A furtive glance around the compartment reassured me that nobody had noticed. What could I do to cheer up, to take my mind off my unhappiness? I had already reread *Toldi* this morning, which Eva had given me as a good-bye gift. And I was feeling too sorry for myself to try talking to Sam or Ida. I still had some of the brown wrapping paper Heinz had given me, so I decided to write a letter to Eva. She would understand how I was feeling. She was as miserable as me. So I smoothed out the wrinkles in the paper, borrowed Father's fountain pen, and began to write.

December 12, 1956
1:00 P.M.

Dear Eva,

Are you surprised to hear from me so soon? I know we only said good-bye this morning, but this trip is boring and I miss you already. The train is packed— people fill every inch of the floor and corridor. The conductor had told us that the entire trip wouldn't last longer than an hour, but it's already been four hours since we left Klosterneuburg and we are still not in Vienna.

To tell you the truth, I'm writing to you so soon after leaving because I'm feeling very scared. I wouldn't admit this to anybody else, except you. I wish I knew where we'll end up living, and if I'll be able to make new friends. I keep remembering that whenever there were any new students in our school at home, the least popular people in our class would make friends with them at first. I wonder if this will happen with us. I have tried to explain what's worrying me to Mother, but she doesn't seem to understand.

You should see what Father did to himself. Whenever I look at him I have to fight an urge to laugh. At home he used to go to the barber shop around the corner from our house every day to be shaved. Well, today he tried shaving himself on the moving train. He looks monstrous! His entire face is full of small cuts. To stop the bleeding, he plastered each cut with a tiny piece of toilet paper. He looks ridiculous.

Mother's brow is creased with worry. She is concerned that we'll have trouble finding a hotel we can afford in Vienna, even though the HIAS gave us a list of cheap places.

Oh, I've got to stop writing now. The train is just pulling into the Vienna railway station.

9:30 P.M.

Well, Eva, Mother was right as usual. You can't imagine the trouble we had finding accomodations. The Gabors found a room in the first hotel on our list, but we had to walk forever before we found the Hotel Johann Strauss on Strauss Street. All four of us are now squeezed into a tiny room on the top floor. The room is plain, but very clean. When we leave the blinds up we can see a giant Ferris wheel turning in the distance. The music sounds tinny on the winter air. Ida wants to ride on the Ferris wheel, but Father says that we don't have enough money. There's a nice little restaurant across the street from our hotel called Matilda's Café. Matilda is a Hungarian name. I'll find out tomorrow if the owner can speak Hungarian, since we're going there for breakfast. It would be nice to be able to speak our language to strangers once again.

You're never going to believe what a shocking discovery I've made, but I swear it's true. There is a black box in the hotel lobby. At certain times of the day, movies appear on it, just by turning a knob. It's like having a movie theatre right inside your own house. I can't understand what the movie characters are saying, because they're all talking in German. We learned that the box is called a television, but everybody refers to it as "the TV".

Are you homesick, Eva? I am. Ida, too. Father says that we should feel lucky that we're finally free. But, somehow, being free doesn't make me feel any different. I just miss my school, my house, and everybody at home. We have no home, no beds of our own, and no money. In so many ways, I felt freer at home.

Well, I'd better finish. Father says my light is keeping the whole family awake. He promised to mail this letter first thing in the morning. I hope it'll reach you before you leave Klosterneuburg. Give my love to Sis.

Your friend forever,
Nelly

10

In Vienna

Matilda's Café was a homey little place with red-checkered tablecloths and lace curtains on the windows. They reminded me of the ones hanging on my window at home, and I became homesick just looking at them. I was right about Matilda. She was born in Hungary, but had lived in Vienna most of her life. She could still speak Hungarian, although she had an accent.

We had been feeling so cooped up living in a hotel room that Matilda's Café quickly became our second home. Matilda claimed that she was famous all over Vienna for her Wiener schnitzel and her apple strudel. I wished we could taste these dishes, but Father only ordered vegetable soup and rolls for supper. It was good, healthy food, but I was so sick of having the same thing day after day.

We spent most of our time walking around the city. The streets were broad and clean and the roads were full of cars. Our drab clothes looked drabber still compared to the stylish people on the streets. We spent our days visiting different embassies to find out which countries were accepting Hungarian refugees. The rest of the time we spent at Matilda's. Ida and I drank her hot chocolate, while Mother and Father had endless cups of fragrant espresso coffee. Even Ida knew better by now than to ask for anything more.

Our first week in Vienna had flown by. I found myself thinking less about what everyone was doing at home— it all seemed so far away. Father had gone to the HIAS offices early this morning, hoping to meet friends from home. Mother, Ida, and I were having breakfast at Matilda's and awaiting his return.

Father was late and, when he did arrive, it was obvious that something had upset him. He barely said hello to Ida or me before drawing Mother aside to speak to her in a low voice. Ida was too busy chattering to Matilda to pay much attention, but I strained to listen. Father was speaking so quietly that I had to edge closer to hear him.

"What's the matter, Vili?" Mother asked him anxiously.

Father said nothing at first. He was rocking on his heels, a sure sign that he was agitated. He seemed unable to meet Mother's eye.

"I know you too well, Vili. Something is definitely bothering you. Were the HIAS officials rude to you? What's the matter?"

Father didn't look up. He was folding his beret into four equal squares, over and over again. He finally raised his head, glancing first at Ida and then at me. He seemed reassured by Ida's chatter and convinced by my efforts to look absorbed in *Toldi*.

"They offered us charity, Kati," he mumbled.

"Oh no, Vili. You must have misunderstood. They only meant to help," Mother said, taking hold of Father's hands.

"I know, I know, but still . . . They were quite insistent. Of course, I refused. You know my temper, Kati. I told the office clerk that we weren't beggars. I was so rude that she was almost in tears. She said she was only doing her job."

"Poor girl. She meant well."

"I know, I know. I was so ashamed that I finally accepted some vouchers for new shoes, just to make her feel better. Somehow it didn't seem as bad as accepting money. Oh, I wish I could get a job in Austria. I'd do anything! Dig ditches, sweep streets—anything at all. But nobody will hire me when I tell them that we're only here temporarily."

"You're too proud, Vili," Mother said. "At least we'll have new shoes for the winter."

"My ever-practical Kati." Father shook his head. "You're right, of course, but that doesn't make it any easier to swallow my pride."

And I wished that I had minded my own business. I couldn't stand to see Father so unhappy. I had to do something to help. I racked my brains all afternoon for ideas, until I remembered Heinz. Now I had a plan. I waited until after dinner had been served in the restaurant and Matilda had sat down for coffee.

"Matilda, could I talk to you for a minute, please? It's private."

"Of course, Nelly. Come into the kitchen. We won't be interrupted there." She winked at me reassuringly and I followed her into the kitchen. She sat down at a table and looked at me expectantly. "What can I do for you?"

Suddenly, I was at a loss for words. Where should I start? I took a deep breath.

"I guess you know that we never order anything expensive on the menu, only vegetable soup and rolls."

"It doesn't matter. Maybe I . . ."

"Please, let me finish." I was determined to go on. "Father can't find any kind of work in Austria, so we have to be very careful with our money. We have already used up much of what he received when he sold his watch. And we were afraid to bring anything else with us from home. Not even my great-grandmother's bracelet that Mother got back after the war. So you see, we have nothing else to sell. I'd like to do something to help. I thought that if we could eat some of your Wiener schnitzel and apple strudel and other kinds of meals instead of only soup every day, we might feel better."

"Well, I think I could arrange that," Matilda said.

"No, no, you don't understand. I'm not asking for charity. I helped out in the kitchen in Klosterneuburg for two weeks. I could do the same for you. I'm a very good dishwasher. If you'd let me wash the dishes in the restaurant, you wouldn't have to pay me, but maybe you could let us order better meals for the price of the vegetable soup."

Matilda was quiet for so long I was convinced she would refuse my proposition. "Well, what a good idea!" she finally said. "I don't need a dishwasher, but I do need a hostess, someone to show the customers to their tables. You know, Nelly, I think you've picked up enough German by now to be able to do the job without any trouble at all."

"Oh, yes, thank you! I'd rather be a hostess than a dishwasher any day."

"I don't blame you," Matilda said with a laugh. "Do your parents know you were planning to talk to me?"

"No. I wanted to see what you'd say first."

"Listen, Nelly, let me handle this my own way. I'll talk to your mother and father."

Later, I noticed Matilda in conversation with my parents. When we returned to our room at the end of the evening, Father asked me to sit down because he had something important to ask me.

"As you know, Nelly, Matilda has been very kind to us," Father said.

"She's a nice lady."

"Yes, she is. And she has asked for a favor from us, a rather unusual request. Normally, I would have refused immediately, but she's been so kind that I wanted to speak to you before deciding. It seems that Matilda's hostess at the restaurant is off work, tending to a sick aunt. The woman is a good employee who wants her job back as soon as her aunt's health improves. In the meantime, Matilda is so busy cooking that she doesn't have time to show customers to their tables. And her waitress is already too overworked to do anything more. Matilda knows we won't be in Vienna long enough for you to go to school here, so she asked me if you would like to be her hostess while we're in the city. She thinks you may want to keep busy. I told her that it's entirely up to you, and I'd ask how you feel about working for her—for free, of course—as a favor to a friend. But she insists that if she can't pay you, she'll reduce the price of our dinners instead. What do you think, Nelly? You don't have to do this if you don't want to."

Hooray! I got the job! I chose my words carefully. "Matilda is right, Father. You can't imagine how I hate just sitting around with nothing to do all day. I'd love to be her hostess."

"Then it's settled," Father said. "Tomorrow morning you can tell Matilda that you have decided to help her out."

From the next day on, between five and eight o'clock every evening, I made sure that my hair was smooth, my braids were neat, and my hands were clean as I took my post by the front entrance of Matilda's Café to welcome dinner guests and show them to their tables. In a few days I learned enough German to be able to greet all the regular customers. My parents and Ida waited until I finished working every evening, and then we had our supper together. Our meals consisted of Matilda's best dishes, for she insisted that I was such a great help to her that she was getting a real bargain. I can't really claim that Wiener schnitzel and apple strudel were making my parents and Ida happier, but at least we were eating better.

We were dwellers in a strange world. I can't say that this was unpleasant. It's just that I wasn't feeling like myself. It was as if I were standing outside of my body watching everything that was happening as if it were happening to someone else.

On a frosty morning three weeks after our arrival in Vienna, I was standing in front of a patisserie across the street from the HIAS offices waiting for my parents and Ida to return. My mouth was watering at the sight of the creamy cakes. I was startled to see my reflection in the shop window. The same face as always was staring back at me—the same eyes, the same lips, even the same fat nose. Yet the Nelly in the window seemed so different from her Hungarian self. The Hungarian Nelly was always laughing, always doing something important with her friends. This Nelly in the window, this stranger Nelly I had become, felt as if she were floating anchorless, with no school, no friends, no belongings, no home.

A tap on my shoulder made me jump. "Imagine running into you like this." It was Janos Selye. He hugged me. Janos was the only one among father's cousins to survive the concentration camps in the war. He was accompanied by his wife, Maria, their ten-year-old son, David, and Maria's father, Natan Kocsis.

"Where are your parents?" he asked.

"In the HIAS offices. They'll be here soon. And they'll be happy to see you."

We settled at one of the little patisserie tables and my

parents and Ida joined us a few minutes later. After they'd greeted each other, Father asked the customary questions among refugees: "Have you decided what to do yet? Do you know where you're going?" For us, the future is a place that keeps changing shape.

"I'd like to go to New Zealand," Father said. "With all the sheep there, they must need veterinarians. But Kati says that New Zealand is at the end of the world, too far from Europe." Mother was not the only one who thought that—I felt the same way.

"New Zealand! We're going to Canada. There are many opportunities there," Janos answered. "You should come to Canada, too. I've heard it's an agricultural country with lots of cattle. You shouldn't have trouble getting a job there, Vili."

"Canada? Where exactly is Canada?" I asked Father.

"Canada is a huge country, just north of the United States, in North America," Father explained.

"The world's first quintuplets were born in Canada just before the war. It was all over the newsreels," Mother said.

"What are quintuplets?" Ida asked.

"Five babies born to the same parents at the same time," Mother explained to her. "Vili," she said, turning back to Father, "perhaps going to Canada would be a good idea if you could get work there. North America is much closer to home than New Zealand."

"Are all of you out of your minds?" Mr. Kocsis said. "I've heard that Canada is terribly cold. Why, you have to put your winter boots on in September over there, and you can't take them off until July. I won't live in

Canada. I'm going to Australia. It has a much better climate."

"I know that Canada has a cold climate," Father said, "but Australia is almost as far away as New Zealand. It sounds as if Canada is the right place for us." As I listened to him, it occured to me that it had been a good idea to stuff my pockets full of mittens before we escaped from Hungary.

I was amazed that such a momentous decision, a decision that would affect the rest of our lives, had been made so impulsively, with so little thought.

A week later, we were being interviewed by officials of the Canadian embassy in Vienna. Father was assured that he could easily find a job in his profession in Canada. All those cattle must need veterinarians to take care of them. An embassy doctor examined us and we were tested for tuberculosis. The next day, we had to go to the Vienna police headquarters, where Mother and Father were fingerprinted to ensure they weren't international criminals. We all tried very hard to look honest when our passport pictures were taken, but Father still looked like a hard-boiled criminal in his photograph. Our pictures weren't much better. Nevertheless, we were issued international passports, which would allow us to enter Canada.

Two weeks later, we said a tearful good-bye to Matilda, and loaded our shabby suitcase onto a bus to Eisenstadt. Once there, we would have to stay in another refugee camp for a fortnight. Next, we had another long and unpleasant train journey to Italy, to the immigrant barracks in the harbor of Genoa. At long last, we were notified to report the next morning to the dock of the ocean liner *Venezuela*, which would transport us to Canada. The Gabors had also received permission to sail, and they would be accompanying us. We should have been tremendously happy—we were finally on our way! But, of course, there was a problem.

11

The *Venezuela*

We were in Genoa, but it might as well have been Klosterneuburg or Eisenstadt. We had been wearing the same clothes, even the same underwear, day after day. The routine of line-ups for food and the communal bath was the same. I felt as if we had been refugees forever.

One morning a few weeks ago, when we were still in Eisenstadt, I had woken up early feeling groggy and hot. As I tiptoed out of the dark room, I was careful not to wake up the rest of the family. But when I looked into the bathroom mirror I screamed.

"What's the matter, Nelly? What's wrong with you?" cried Mother.

"Come quickly! I'm completely covered in spots!" I looked in the mirror again with horror.

Mother rushed in and carefully examined me, Frankenstein's monster reborn. My face, my body, my hands and feet, even my fingers and toes, were covered with small red spots. "It looks like the rash Ida had when she caught chickenpox last year," Mother said.

The doctor in charge of the Eisenstadt immigrant camp confirmed it—I had chickenpox. At age thirteen, I had caught a children's disease. I was humiliated! For almost two weeks I was in isolation in our room, with no children allowed to come near me. My rash dried up gradually. By the time we received our notice to sail, I was no longer infectious. But I looked even worse than before, with my entire face and body covered by dried-up little sores. Even though I looked awful, I was beginning to let myself feel joy. I felt like a prisoner liberated from jail as I began packing for our ocean voyage. I was filled with hope when I thought of lying in my own bed in a room where I wasn't afraid to turn off the lights, knowing the shadows on the wall as if they were old friends. I was eager to be in a place where the night noises of creaking floorboards and the street outside my window were so familiar they offered only comfort.

The immigrant barracks were located right by the harbor, so it only took us five minutes to reach the *Venezuela*'s dock. The gray ocean liner rested like a huge metal whale in the harbor. A uniformed sailor greeted us at the small bridge leading aboard. He spoke Hungarian, even though all the crew were Italians. I looked awful and I didn't want any strangers to see me, so I stood right behind Father to be blocked from view. We had entered that state of travel where things seem to unfold of their own accord. The sailor checked our papers and nodded pleasantly.

"Welcome to the *Venezuela*, folks," he said with a smile. "I hope you'll enjoy your trip with us. Marco will show you to your cabin." He called over a steward to help us with our bags. I was still standing right behind Father, keeping out of sight. But when Father bent down to hand over our luggage to the steward, the sailor checking our papers noticed me for the first time.

"What's wrong with the girl?" he barked.

"Nothing at all," Father said. "She's been ill, but she is fine now."

"What's that rash on her face?"

"She had chickenpox, but she isn't infectious anymore," Mother explained.

"How do you know? Did a doctor see her? Do you have a doctor's certificate that she is healthy?"

"She was examined by the camp physician in Eisenstadt and he ordered her to be in isolation," Father said. "We didn't take her to a doctor in Genoa because she is feeling much better. Our younger daughter had chickenpox last year so we know what to expect. Nelly isn't infectious anymore."

By now, the sailor was tapping his chin with his pencil. Finally, he said, "I'm sorry, but I can't let you board until your daughter is completely recovered. I have to think of the welfare of the other passengers on the ship."

"I understand that, but Nelly is fine." Father said.

"I'm sorry, I can't take the responsibility," he replied.

"Why don't you get the ship's doctor to examine her," Father suggested. "I'm certain he'll pronounce her healthy."

"Unfortunately, Dr. Marciano won't be joining us until tomorrow, just before departure. I can't hold your cabin until then. We have too many families on the waiting list. But don't worry, the next ship sails two weeks from now. We'll try to get you on it."

We had been waiting such a long time to get on with our lives. Now, so close to the end, patience evaporated. We were frantic.

"We've already been waiting for several weeks. We want to begin our new lives in Canada." Father looked and sounded desperate. Mother was quietly weeping and Ida was rocking back and forth on her heels, sucking her thumb.

"I'm sorry, there's nothing I can do. I'll have to ask you to wait by the side, here, until I can clear the bridge so you can return to land."

He turned back to the line of passengers waiting to board the *Venezuela*, and we had no choice but to put our sparse luggage in a corner of the reception area of the ship. It was a large room that resembled the lobby of a hotel. A wide staircase along the back wall led to the upper and lower decks. People were rushing back and forth purposefully. Everyone had somewhere to go, except for us.

"I don't want to stand here," Ida said. She had a worried expression on her face. Nobody answered her.

I felt horribly guilty, although I realized that none of

this was my fault. I had to do something to stop them from throwing us off the ship. But what?

"There's nothing we can do but wait. A few weeks more won't make a difference," Father said in hearty tones that did not ring true. "It's unfortunate that they don't have a doctor aboard. But I see their point. They have too many people waiting. We can't expect them to reserve space for us until the doctor can see you."

Just then, I noticed the steward at the bridge talking to the Gabors. They had no problems being processed and I watched Dr. Gabor and Sam gather up their suitcases and Mrs. Gabor put their passports back into her purse. I realized that I had to make my move immediately.

"Father," I said, tugging at his sleeve, "Dr. Gabor was our family doctor at home. Why can't he tell them that I am no longer contagious?"

"Smart girl!" Father said. "It's certainly worth a try." And he hurried off to speak to the sailor before the Gabors left for their cabin.

The sailor agreed to allow him to examine me, and Dr. Gabor pronounced me healthy and non-contagious. The ship's doctor agreed with this diagnosis when he checked me over the next day, an hour before sailing.

Our quarters in the hold of the ship were in a tiny cabin with two bunk beds and a small table flanked by two tiny armchairs. There was also a minuscule bathroom attached with a toilet, sink, and shower. We could see out through a porthole just above the water line.

"This is like a doll's house! How can we all fit in here?" Ida asked.

"I don't care if it's small. I just don't care," Mother said while trying to twirl around in the cramped space. She looked like a young girl. "For the first time since we left home I can believe that we'll be able to lead normal lives once again." She gave me a big hug.

"Will the voyage be long?" Ida asked.

"It'll take just under two weeks to reach the port of Halifax," Father explained to her. "From there, we'll take the train to Montreal, in the province of Quebec. It's supposed to be a wonderful city. Canada is a big and beautiful country."

My parents were happy that their friends were also traveling on the *Venezuela*. The Gabors' cabin was next-door, and the Selyes were down the hall. So I was stuck with Sam and my cousin David for the entire trip. To be honest, I didn't really mind Sam traveling with us anymore. I had changed my mind about him in Klosterneuburg. I had to admit that although Sam still annoyed me sometimes, he was agreeable most of the time, and could actually be a lot of fun. Also, I had noticed lately that he had become very good-looking. He had grown a lot the last few months and was a head taller than me. It was nice to be with a boy who didn't make me feel like a gorilla. He had curly blond hair and the nicest green eyes behind his glasses. It was embarrassing that he was always trying to please me. He got red in the face whenever my arm brushed against his, or if he accidentally leaned close to me.

My cousin David Selye was a different story. Neither Ida nor I could stand him. He was the biggest bully imaginable, although you'd never know it by looking at him.

He was about the skinniest boy I had ever seen despite his mother's obsession with feeding him. Even Mother's eyes glazed over whenever Maria began to explain that David was a "finicky eater". The truth of the matter was that David was usually too busy being obnoxious to take the time to eat. He was always very proper and polite with adults, but not all of them were fooled.

"I don't trust that boy," Father said. "It's unnatural for a child to be so polite."

Mother always jumped to David's defense. "Don't be so critical, Vili. You know Maria. It's not the child's fault that she insists on such formal manners."

What Mother didn't know was that David possessed a Jekyll-and-Hyde personality. The minute the adults left the room the polite, passive boy disappeared and the rude and mean David emerged. When I was told that he would be sailing with us I decided to have as little to do with him as possible, but Mother had other ideas.

Ida and I finished unpacking quickly and decided to explore the ship.

"Let's get Sam to come along," Ida said. He was nice to her. Although he did tease her, it was in a gentle way, and he wasn't cruel like a lot of boys his age might have been.

"Fine with me. Let's knock on his cabin door."

"Just a minute," Mother said. "You have to ask David, too. It's the kind thing to do. Also, Nelly, make sure that Ida doesn't go near the railing. We'll be in the dining salon if you need us."

Wonderful! Not only was I to be saddled with David, I also had to babysit Ida.

The four of us climbed the steep staircase leading to the deck of the ship. For a glorious moment I dreamed of pushing David overboard, just to hear the sailors cry "Man overboard!" But I knew better than to try anything. David would probably have drowned just to spite me.

"Look what I've got," he said. He reached into his pocket and pulled out an army knife with a curved silver blade.

"Where did you get that?" I asked him.

"Put it away before you hurt somebody," Sam warned.

"My father got it for me in Genoa. He says all boys should carry pocket knives. Girls aren't allowed to have them."

Ida took the bait. "They are too!" she cried. "I could have a knife if I wanted it, but I don't want one. Pocket knives are completely useless."

"My knife isn't useless! You're just jealous. I can do lots of things with it. Why, I could even stab you with my knife if I wanted to." He pointed the weapon at my sister.

"No you couldn't," I told him. "You'd get into the biggest trouble of your life if you did something like that."

"I dare you to do it!" Ida challenged, holding out her left arm to him. I snickered. David was still for a second and then, to my utter horror, he plunged the tip of the blade into Ida's arm. Blood spurted out. Her mouth formed an astonished O.

Ida was too shocked at first even to cry. She just stood still holding her arm. She became so pale that I was afraid she would faint. I put my arm around her and helped her to lower herself to the deck. Sam immediately knocked David down and pounded his face with his fists. A steward came running to investigate the commotion and separated them with a great deal of difficulty. The shock of David's attack was wearing off and Ida's arm had stopped bleeding. She struggled to her feet and, looking furious and still a little dazed, she followed the steward into the dining salon. Everyone in the room crowded around us, asking what had happened. Ida stood patiently while Father examined her arm.

"It's just a superficial wound. She doesn't need any stitches," he said. Janos was furious with David. He took away the knife and ordered his son to apologize to Ida. David began to whine.

"It's not my fault! Ida told me to do it. She dared me to stab her! Tell them that you did! Nelly, tell them that she did!"

"Fool!" Sam said contemptuously.

"Did you dare David to stab you, Ida?" Mother asked.

"It wasn't like that. We were just teasing him. . . ."

"Did you?" Mother repeated sternly.

"I didn't mean it," cried Ida. "I didn't think for a moment that he'd do something so stupid."

"I didn't, either," I told Mother.

"Quiet, girls!" Mother said sternly. "Well, Maria, it seems the girls did tease David. But I think a ten-year-old boy ought to have better judgment than to go around hurting people with his knife."

"Oh, you know what boys are. . . . David is so

high-spirited. The girls shouldn't have provoked him," Maria replied, ruffling David's hair.

I could see by the high color in Mother's face that she was furious at Maria's reply. "I think it's time to call it a night and return to our cabins," Father quickly interjected before Mother could answer her.

Back in our quarters, Father calmed Mother down before he turned to us. "We don't think you were responsible for what happened. But, please, don't tease David again. Just stay away from him as much as possible."

It was impossible to follow Father's suggestion on a ship with only a few children our age for companionship. The next day David followed us around for so long that we finally gave in and let him stay with us. No one ever talked about the stabbing incident again but, whenever David became particularly unbearable, Ida or I pointed to the small scar on her forearm. David always pretended that he didn't know what we were doing, but he would start behaving better afterward.

It didn't seem as if we were even moving. There was only the dark ocean, the dark boat, and the moaning winds that chilled us to the bone. A person could only jog around the deck so many times and, after the first thousand games, shuffle-board no longer seemed fun. By the afternoon of our fourth day aboard the ship I had reread my taped-up copy of *Toldi* two more times. We tried browsing in the ship's gift shop, but the sour saleswoman shooed us away. I found myself sitting on the deck flipping a coin hour after hour. To make things worse, Ida had been getting on my nerves. She always wanted to tag along with me, asking me to play with her. An hour ago, while she was in the bathroom, I had finally been able to escape to the ship's library to write a letter to Miki. I knew it would be only a matter of time before she found me, so I would have to write quickly. I stared and stared at the paper in front of me, but no words flowed from my pen. I didn't have this problem when I wrote to Sari and Eva. I had had so much to say to them that my pen had trouble keeping up with my thoughts. If I were honest with myself, I would have to admit that I hadn't even thought of Miki lately. But I had asked Sari in my letter to her to tell Miki that I would be writing to him soon, and I believed in keeping a promise. So I began.

Feb. 17, 1957
5:00 P.M.

Dear Miki,

I'm sorry that I haven't written to you before, but we've been moving about so much that I haven't had a spare minute . . .

I put down my pen. I sounded so dumb! Miki would know immediately that I was lying. I crumpled up the paper and began again.

Feb. 17, 1957
5:00 P.M.

Dear Miki,

I bet you're surprised to hear from me. I hope you're well . . .

What should I say next? I nibbled on my pen, but no new ideas appeared on the paper. Ida arrived at the library door, and I was relieved to see her.

"What are you doing?" she asked.

"Oh, nothing," I told her as I folded up the letter and put it into my pocket.

"Mother sent me to get you. She asked Father to take us to the gift shop to give us something to do."

Ida and I found Father quickly and went with him to the store. This time the saleswoman greeted us with a smile on her lips, but we were not fooled. She was the same bad-tempered person who had shooed us away when we were playing on the deck in front of her store. Ida stuck out her tongue as soon as she turned her back.

"May I help you?" she asked in German.

"My daughters would like to buy something," Father explained.

"Please, look around. See if you can find something you like. And let me know if I can be of assistance," she said, her voice dripping with sweetness. I looked at her with contempt. She pretended not to notice.

The prices in the shop were very high, but Father insisted that we buy something. Ida quickly chose a small plastic doll. She missed the doll she had left propped up on her pillow in Hungary when we left home. I couldn't decide between a tablecloth that had to be embroidered in a cross-stitch with brightly colored silks, and a pretty bracelet made of shells of different sizes. The embroidery would make a wonderful present for my parents' wedding anniversary next month, but the bracelet was so beautiful! Each of the little shells, so perfect, tinkled as I moved my arm. I was not going to ask Father to buy both. Each item was more expensive than Ida's doll. I decided to be practical. So, with a sigh of regret, I returned the bracelet to the shelf.

"I'll take the embroidery, Father."

"What's wrong with the bracelet?" Father asked. "It's very pretty. Don't you like it?"

"Oh, I do! It's beautiful, but far too expensive."

"Let me worry about the cost," Father said. He turned to the saleswoman and handed her both the embroidery and the bracelet. "We'll take both," he told her, and slipped the bracelet onto my wrist. I checked my reflection in the mirror hanging by the cash register. What a difference the bracelet made. As soon as I put it on, it was no longer the shabby, immigrant Nelly staring back at me. Why, I looked almost pretty, as I used to in Hungary.

Ida called her new doll Jutka, in honor of her favorite doll in Veszprem. The new Jutka was much smaller, and her body and face were made of stiff plastic. Ida insisted that Jutka was so pretty it didn't matter that she didn't have real hair or that she couldn't open and close her eyes like the Hungarian Jutka. The doll's nakedness bothered her, but doll clothes cost a lot.

"It's no fun playing with a naked doll," Ida whined to Mother. "You can't do anything with a naked doll."

"Let's see what I can find in my suitcase," Mother told her. She rummaged through her meager luggage and finally pulled out a pair of manicure scissors and the large orange-and-green scarf she had worn the day we escaped. She held up the scarf in the same way a magician would display a rabbit he pulled from a hat.

"This is great material for doll clothes," she said. Ida was thrilled.

"Oh, Mother, it's the only scarf you've got. You can't just give it away. It's very cold in Canada," I said.

"Don't worry, my dear, my coat buttons up high, so I don't really need a scarf. And we can't allow poor Jutka to be cold. Don't you agree that she'll look smashing in a sari?" With deft hands she cut the material in two, and wrapped a piece around the doll's body, creating a sari. The second piece became a turban.

Ida loved the new clothes. She thought her doll looked beautiful in them. She spent hours wrapping and unwrapping the costume, and putting Jutka to bed in a shoebox provided by our steward. But, a few days later, tragedy struck! She accidentally dropped Jutka while playing with her. The doll split in half, along the two plastic seams running down her sides. Mother saved the day again, this time by wrapping an elastic band tightly around the doll's neck and waist. When Jutka was wearing her costume, it was almost impossible to see the elastic.

Last night I dreamed I was riding a roller coaster in Vienna. Up and down, climbing, plunging, over and over again until I became nauseated and dizzy. Mother woke me by turning on the cabin light, and I realized that I wasn't in an amusement park but in the middle of the Atlantic Ocean aboard a ship during a violent thunderstorm. We could hear the raging of the wind and, through the porthole, we could see the splashing of the black waves, which obscured our view of the angry ocean.

"I feel awful," Mother moaned, holding her hands over her stomach. "I think I'm going to be sick."

"I do, too," I told her. "I feel like I'm going to die." The night passed in a sick haze. Ida's incessant "Is the ship going to sink?" drove me mad. She couldn't be convinced that everything would be fine.

All of us looked like wax figures the next morning. Mother declared that even a bite of food would kill her. Both she and I wanted to be left alone to suffer in peace. Father would have none of that.

"Don't be silly, girls," he said. "All you need is some fresh air. I'll settle you on the deck, while Ida and I go for breakfast." The storm had had a similar effect on most of our fellow travelers and, although it was only nine o'clock in the morning, all of the lounge chairs were occupied. The best we could do was to spread out our blankets on the deck. We were only halfway through the voyage and I was filled with dread at the thought of feeling this way for the rest of the trip.

Fortunately, I did start to feel better, but poor Mother felt nauseated at the slightest motion of the ship. Father planned to get up at six o'clock every morning to reserve a deck chair for her.

I knew how much Father loved to sleep late, so the next morning before dawn, I bundled up for the freezing winter weather in the layers of clothes I had worn during our escape and offered to take his place on deck. It was very early, and I was still so tired that I could barely drag myself up the steep staircase. I was surprised to find Sam already on deck before me.

"Hi Nelly," he said, "we're the early birds of the ship today."

"I couldn't sleep, so I thought I'd let Father stay in bed a little longer," I told him.

"I came up here fifteen minutes ago to hold a deck chair for my dad. He is constantly throwing up."

"How disgusting!"

Sam pulled two deck chairs closer to reserve them. For some reason, I couldn't think of anything to say to him, so I concentrated on the monotonous roaring of the dark sea, the splashing of the angry waves against the boat's hull, and the shrill screams of the seagulls.

"What a terrible day," I finally stammered. "Gray ocean, gray sky, gray ship—everything's gray." Just then, the rising sun peeped out from behind the clouds. I had to put my hand above my eyes to shield them from the sudden glare. Scanning the endless horizon, I thought the sea seemed to go on forever. There was something waiting for us beyond what I could see. But what? Another home? Friends? Our own beds? Oh, how I missed what I had left behind. The rapid swaying of the boat made me feel as if I were floating in space, rudderless, belonging nowhere.

Sam and I were sitting close to each other, and I noticed that his eyelashes were very long and curly around his green eyes. I didn't want him to know I was staring at him, so I forced myself to look away. We talked awkwardly like strangers.

"Don't you think that David is the biggest idiot you've ever met?" Sam asked.

"Definitely! I'm so angry he is traveling with us to Montreal. Father told me your family is heading to Winnipeg. I've heard it's extremely cold there."

"I know. I've heard that, too. But my mother has cousins there, and they have a son my age."

"That's wonderful. I'm sure you'll like him, and Winnipeg too. I just hope that Montreal will be nice."

"Do you know if Winnipeg is very far from Montreal, Nelly?"

"Oh, yes, it's far—thousands of kilometers away. Father showed me a map of Canada yesterday. It's a very large country."

"So I guess we won't be able to see each other." Sam's voice was low and sad. I realized with mild surprise that I also felt sad. I kept my eyes on the waves as if I had never seen them before. The dark winter dawn wrapped us in icy solitude.

"Do you ever think of your friends back home?" Sam asked.

"Yes, I do. But a little less than when I first left. I miss Sari the most."

"And Miki?" I was so startled at his question that I actually met his gaze. His expression was determined.

"Miki? No, I hardly ever think of him now."

"Do you miss him?" Sam persisted.

"No, I don't. Not anymore," I answered without hesitation. And I realized that I was telling him the complete truth. "I promised to write to Miki, and I tried, but I didn't know what to say." I pulled the letter I had started in the library out of my pocket.

Sam took the letter and folded it into the shape of a paper airplane. "Do you want to see if this plane can fly?" he asked.

"Sure! Let's try it out."

Sam leaned over the ship's railing and threw the paper airplane into the air. It soared gracefully for a moment on the bitter wind before being swallowed by the frothing waves.

Sam smiled. "It was a good airplane," he said. "But, Nelly, I'm really sorry that we won't be living in the same city when we get to Canada. I'll miss you a lot. We should write to each other."

"I'd like that."

"I'll give you our cousin's address. He'll forward your letters to me. And you can let me know your address later," Sam said.

He looked so dejected that I gathered up all my courage and took his hand in mine. We sat in silence, holding hands and listening to the music of the waves until we heard Father climbing the staircase to relieve me.

Father was very surprised when I offered to reserve Mother's deck chair for her every morning. Being Father, he was immediately suspicious of my motives. "What are you up to?" he asked. "Why are you so eager to get up at dawn?" Because I didn't know how to answer him, I pretended not to hear him. When he noticed Mother signaling him with one of her special looks, he stopped asking questions.

For the rest of the trip, Sam and I met at six o'clock every morning. When I was with him I felt carefree and happy, like I used to be back home. I couldn't remember a time when I hadn't liked him—a lot.

Even though I was not infectious from chickenpox anymore, I was still weak and tired. When Dr. Marciano examined me at the beginning of our ocean voyage, he had suggested that I should take a nap in our cabin every day after lunch while my family was walking on the deck or playing cards in one of the smoky salons.

Today was the ninth day of our trip, and my ninth nap. I was tossing and turning on my bunk, unable to sleep. Suddenly, clanging bells and a deafening siren shattered the silence. I jumped out of bed and rushed to the cabin door, opening it a crack to peek out. All I could see were crew members in life jackets, running up and down the staircase at the end of the hall. The sirens kept wailing. I dashed up to a sailor passing by and grabbed hold of his sleeve.

"Is the ship sinking?" I asked him. "Please, tell me what's going on!" He shook off my hand, shouted something in Italian, and rushed off.

The hall was empty by now. The bells kept on ringing loudly. My God! Was the ship sinking? I didn't know what to do. Where were Mother and Father? Had they forgotten me? I hurried back to the cabin in cold terror.

The siren was still wailing insistently. I had to save myself somehow. I was freezing, even though the cabin was stuffy. I told myself not to panic. Mother, Father, and Ida must be in the lifeboats already. How could they have left me?

Fear dried my mouth and constricted my throat. Fear

took hold of my hands, making them shake so badly that I could hardly pull on my coat and a knit cap. The life jackets were buried below our suitcases on a low shelf. I struggled into one with a great deal of difficulty. Oh, why hadn't I paid attention when the steward demonstrated how to put it on? The lifeboats were on deck. I had to reach them somehow. I had to save myself. I remembered to put on my mittens. The sea was ice cold.

I opened the cabin door again. Still, nobody was around. I was all alone. Had everybody forgotten me? I started up the staircase. Suddenly, I realized that something was different from before. Ah! The silence! The alarm had stopped and the bells were no longer ringing. Mother appeared at the top of the stairs. She was smiling and chatting with Ida who was skipping by her side. They were both startled to see me dressed in a life jacket.

"Nelly, my dear, what's going on?" Mother asked. "Why are you out of bed? Why are you in your life jacket?"

I was afraid to speak in case I started to cry. I rushed up to her, wrapped my arms around her waist, and burrowed my face in her neck. "I thought the ship was sinking and you had forgotten me," I was finally able to stammer. "I was coming to find you."

Mother pulled me even closer. "Oh no! It was just a fire drill. We should have warned you. I'm so sorry! But how could you believe that we'd ever leave you behind?"

The terrors of the past months had caught up with me. The old Nelly would have laughed, embarrassed at such a mistake. But this Nelly, this stranger, was inconsolable. Hours passed, and it was time to go to the dining hall. I clung to Mother like a child.

Three days later, Father rose very early, even before me. He looked through the porthole to check the weather, and immediately broke into a great whoop of joy.

"Kati! Children! Wake up! Come here quickly! We've arrived. Look, it's Canada!"

The whole family crowded around the window. "Pick me up! Pick me up! I can't see!" Ida cried. Father scooped her up into his arms, while I stood on my tiptoes. I could finally distinguish in the distance tiny toy houses dotting the snowy coastline.

"Halifax!" Father said. "We should reach it in half an hour. At last, Canada! Our new home."

We had finally arrived.

12

The Train

Another train trip! It was as if I had been traveling all my life. I had become so accustomed to moving about that whenever I saw an airplane flying overhead or train chugging through the countryside I felt I should be on it. I could hardly believe that soon we'd once again be like other people, living in the same place week after week and going to school regularly.

But this trip was different. At long last, we were nearing our final destination—Montreal. It was going to take us a full day and night to reach it. The expensive sleeping coach was out of the question because we had to save our money for food and rent until Father got a job. Mother and Father had difficulty sleeping in a sitting position and were awake all night, but Ida and I curled up in our seats and were able to doze off for short periods of time.

I had grown accustomed to the sound of the rails, but now the continuous motion beat an anxious tattoo. "What's Montreal like?" I asked Father again, hoping for reassurance I knew he couldn't offer. "How soon will we be going to school?" I knew I sounded like a baby, even to myself, but I needed to hear his answers.

"You'll go to school as soon as we get there. Both you and Ida. And about time, too. Stop worrying! I'm certain that you'll love Montreal," Father said. "It's a large city, much bigger than Veszprem. Everybody speaks both French and English."

"Do you think we'll be able to do the work at school? We can't speak either of those languages. How will we know what's going on?"

"Maybe you won't understand everything at the beginning, but you'll soon catch on."

Father didn't seem to understand what was bothering me, but he listened to me patiently. "How am I going to talk to the other children if I can't understand what they're saying?" I asked him.

"Don't worry. You've already picked up English phrases in Halifax. And you can understand even more than you can speak. It's Mother and I who might have a problem."

"How much longer before we'll get to Montreal?" Ida asked, restlessly shifting in her seat.

Mother's eyes were closed as she answered. "We still have over half a day of travel ahead of us."

"I hate this stupid train. I'm so tired." Like me, Ida

seemed younger than when we had left Veszprem. She whined like a little child.

"I don't blame you," Father said. "I keep checking my watch every five minutes." He stared unseeing at the gray countryside.

"Can you think of something else for me to do?" Ida swung her legs to the floor and sat up. Mother had already had her counting cars on passing trains.

Now she had a suggestion. "How about going out for tea by yourselves?" she asked. "You could go to the dining car for afternoon tea, like grown-ups. But you'd better tidy up first."

I tried to smooth out the creases in my pleated navy skirt, but it was beyond help. It was too short, but it fit looser in the waist than it used to at home. My blue sweater was also skimpy and stretched uncomfortably across my back.

Ida complained bitterly that her gray wool dress rode up under her arms. She tugged at her sleeves, trying to pull them down with no success. Her dress was very short, too. She was all knobby arms and legs. She yelped in pain when I tried to untangle her hair with Mother's comb. I tidied my own braids, then bit down on my lips and pinched my cheeks. Finally, I was ready for our outing.

Father came with us as far as the dining car at the end of the train, just before the caboose. He pressed a quarter into each of our palms and told us to be back in an hour. The dining car was only half full. Busboys were scurrying about, setting tables covered by crisp white linens with fine white-and-gold china, silver cutlery, and crystal glasses. We felt very grown-up just to be sitting there by ourselves in such elegant surroundings. A gray-haired waiter asked, "Have the young ladies made up their minds yet?"

"Tea," I said grandly, hoping he would understand my English.

"Tea," echoed Ida.

"With milk or lemon?"

"What's he asking?" Ida said to me in our native Hungarian.

"I have no idea."

"Milk or lemon, miss?" the waiter repeated with a twinkle in his eye.

"Yes," I told him in my most adult manner.

"Yes? Would you like milk or lemon with your tea?" He repeated.

"What's he saying?" Ida asked again in Hungarian.

"I have no idea. Milk, lemon," I answered the waiter, imitating what he had said to me.

"Milk, lemon," Ida echoed.

"Both?" The waiter was incredulous.

"Both," I told him, hoping that this was the right answer to the question we didn't understand.

Shrugging his shoulders, the waiter left and came back with a pot of tea, a container of milk, and thin lemon slices prettily arranged on a saucer.

"Why are they serving milk with tea?" Ida asked me. In Hungary we always drank our tea with lemon. Milk was reserved for coffee.

"I guess this is how you're supposed to drink it in Canada. Every country has its own customs."

First, we put the lemon slices into the tea, then we poured in the milk. The milk immediately curdled and we ended up with a disgusting mixture. The busboy snickered, but the waiter hushed him. Not a muscle moved in the waiter's face.

"We can't drink this," Ida said miserably. "It looks horrible."

"Drink it," I whispered to her angrily. "Do you want to make fools of us?"

"I'll bring you another pot of tea," the waiter said, reaching for our cups.

"No, I like," I told him, and picked up my cup, crooking my baby finger in my most sophisticated manner.

"I like," Ida echoed miserably.

The waiter and the busboy were expressionless as we drank the disgusting tea. The waiter didn't let us pay him and even brought us a plate of chocolate-chip cookies at no charge. He explained with a great deal of difficulty that it was the policy of the railroad to provide free refreshments to all children new to Canada.

13

Dear Sam

Finally, we arrived in Montreal. At first we lived in a hotel, but every day Mother and Father went out looking for an apartment we could afford. As soon as we had a real place to live in, Ida and I would go to school.

In the meantime, though, we were stuck in another hotel. This time it was the Hotel Darlington on Van Horne Street. The hotel bedspreads were ragged and the rug was gritty. A huge neon Red Rose Tea sign hung from a building across the street. Both the giant cup of tea and the words "Red Rose" on the billboard appeared and disappeared, appeared and disappeared, time after time, day after day. Ida and I spent hours watching it. We wanted to see if it skipped a turn, but it never did. Neither of us had ever seen anything like it at home.

Before saying good-bye to me in Halifax, Sam had given me his cousins' address in Winnipeg. We promised to write to each other regularly. I already missed him and wanted to let him know all that had happened to us during the last few days. Of course, first I had to solve the usual problem—we still had no money for stationery. After some careful searching in our room, I found a block of writing paper in a desk drawer. I borrowed Father's fountain pen again and, without any further delay, began the longest letter I had ever written.

March 9, 1957
11:00 A.M.

Dear Sam,

I have so much to tell you that I couldn't wait any longer to write. As you can see by my letterhead, we're still living in a hotel. But don't write to me here because we may be gone by the time your letter would reach me.

Do you remember when I told you that Winnipeg was very cold? Well, I must have been thinking about Montreal. People who've been living here a long time claim that this is the coldest winter the city has had in the last thirty years. I can't imagine Winnipeg being any colder. Our coats from Hungary aren't warm enough. I'm freezing most of the time. I wear my mitts, but my fingers are always stiff and sore.

Don't you think that Canada is very different from what we expected? I'm not even sure what I had imagined, I only know that I feel as if I'm in a strange new world and I don't belong.

The morning after we arrived we were afraid to leave the hotel because of the weather, but we were so hungry that we put on layers of sweaters under our coats and went in search of a restaurant. We thought we wouldn't have to walk very far.

The Hotel Darlington is on a street with rows of huge, old apartment blocks interspersed with smaller shops. The whole street was deserted, except for us. It was as if we were in a ghost town. By the time we'd gone a block, we had to cover our noses and ears with our hands. We were desperate for a restaurant or café sign, but we just couldn't find one. Father was so frustrated that he stopped a lone passer-by whose only visible features were watery, dark eyes glistening above a plaid scarf wrapped around the lower part of his face. My parents claim that my English is the most fluent in the family, so I was delegated to talk to him. "Where breakfast . . . café?" I muttered.

The man answered in very quick French and, naturally, we couldn't understand a single word.

"Where? Where?" I persisted. Didn't he understand that he had to reply in English?

"Um, um," Father said, mimicking eating. The man shrugged his shoulders, pointed to the drugstore behind us, and hurried away. Father swore—something he has started to do. "We'd better keep looking."

We walked up and down both sides of the street for several blocks, but there was no sign of a restaurant. "This is crazy," Father said. "Don't Canadians eat?"

By now, we were chilled to the bone, and even our

faces were going numb. "I think we should go into the pharmacy to warm ourselves up," Mother suggested as we once again passed the drugstore the man had pointed to. We opened the door, expecting to step into a place where the druggist dispenses medicines, only to discover it's different in Canada. We saw the pharmacist's dispensing counter. We also saw shelves of cards, perfume, candy and, best of all, a lunch counter.

Even my parents were amazed. "For goodness' sake! Eating in a pharmacy! Now I've seen everything!" Mother exclaimed.

It was lots of fun sitting on the bar stools by the counter. I'd never seen anything like them in Hungary. Ida kept spinning around and around on hers until we thought it would come unscrewed.

Canadian food is so different from our food back home. That morning, we ate toast made of white sandwich bread. It was delicious, and at the same time so different from the dark European rye bread we're used to. We washed the toast down with steaming cups of hot cocoa topped with miniature white marshmallows. I couldn't help thinking what a terrific country this is, where candy is put into breakfast drinks. Mother and Father let me taste their coffee. I found it much weaker than the strong European espresso they drank at home. In my opinion, most Canadians seem friendly. The teenage waitress behind the counter kept smiling at us and, something that would never happen at home, filling up my parents' coffee cups without charging them an extra penny.

I noticed a picture hanging on the wall behind the counter. It was a poster of a young man with a guitar across his chest. We had seen pictures of the same person plastered all over the hotel lobby and in several shop windows. I asked the waitress who he was.

"Who is man?" I said.

"You're kidding me," the girl answered as she wiped her palms on her white apron and blew a gigantic pink bubble with the gum she was chewing. I had never seen anybody do anything like that before. I decided to ask my parents if we could buy some to try to figure out how to do it.

I turned to the girl again. "Man," I repeated, pointing at the poster. "Man famous?" By now, I was feeling pretty good about my English.

"Famous? He's Elvis Presley! You actually don't recognize a picture of Elvis?" the waitress asked me incredulously.

"Elvis? Who is Elvis?" I had never heard of him before.

"He is the world's most famous rock-and-roll singer. Would I ever like to meet him!" the girl said, as she pretended to swoon from joy.

"Who is that man?" Father asked me in Hungarian.

"A rock-and-roll singer." I repeated the English words because I had no idea how to translate them into Hungarian. "I guess it's a person who sings to rolling stones. Why would he want to do that?"

Father was certain that I didn't know what I was

talking about. "You must have misunderstood her, Nelly! That can't be. Nobody is that foolish."

"That's what the girl said," I told him firmly. "You never know what Canadians are up to."

I could see by Father's face that he still wasn't wholly convinced. I couldn't truly blame him, for the waitress's answer was so strange. What do you think, Sam? Aren't Canadian people weird—eating in pharmacies, singing to rocks? And have you noticed that they speak English with such a strange accent that it's nearly impossible to understand them?

Well, I have to stop now. We are going to look at another apartment. I'll try to finish this letter as soon as possible.

March 11, 1957
7:30 P.M.

Well, Sam, here I am again. A lot has happened in the last couple of days. We've started to meet Canadians, and we were invited for dinner at a kosher restaurant close to our hotel by members of a local synagogue. At first, I didn't want to go. I thought it would be all grown-up talk. But in the end, I was glad that I had changed my mind! I've got to tell you what I found out. But let me start at the beginning.

It didn't take us long to get ready, even though this was our first "social engagement", as Mother called it, since we had left Hungary. Mother had washed our clothes in the bathroom sink the night before and spread them over the radiators, giving our room the appearance of a launderette. She couldn't do anything about wrinkling because we didn't have an iron.

I'm glad that none of my friends back home can see me now. Sometimes, when I pass by a mirror and unexpectedly catch my reflection, I don't even recognize the shabby stranger staring back at me. It's always a shock to realize that it's me, Nelly Adler. I'm never quite sure that some of the people we pass on the streets aren't laughing at us for the way we're dressed. No matter how often or how quickly I spin around, I still haven't caught anybody actually laughing at us. Perhaps I'm not quick enough. I don't mind telling you all this, Sam, because you're in the same boat as me. Is it any easier for boys to be immigrants than for girls? I hate being an immigrant, don't you?

My shabby clothes put me in a foul mood as we waited impatiently for our Canadian hosts to pick us up and take us to the restaurant. My spirits lifted when two men finally arrived at our door, and Father was shocked when he looked at the younger of the two. "My God! You've got to be Sandor Berger," he said.

"No, I'm not," the lanky young man replied in broken Hungarian. "I'm Aaron Berger. Sandor is my grandfather, and everybody says I look just like him. He'll be very happy to see you. Both he and my grandmother are waiting for us at the restaurant."

I could see my parents cheering up at the prospect of meeting friends and being able to communicate without the effort of speaking in English. Although Mr. Berger had left Hungary twenty years earlier, Father still remembered the old man coming to his boyhood home to visit with my grandparents. Sandor Berger and Father hit it off immediately. Best of all, Mr. Berger owns a clothing store and he has promised to sell us warmer winter jackets tomorrow. What a luxury it will be to finally be warm.

After dinner we went back to the Bergers' apartment for dessert and coffee. When Mr. Berger saw that we didn't have winter boots, he suggested that we buy some at the downtown Eaton's basement store. They're the cheapest there," he said, "but don't buy anything else. I can sell you everything you need much more reasonably from my own store."

While we were having dessert, Mr. Berger talked about his synagogue and Passover in the spring. He invited us to spend it with them. Then he told us that his grandchildren attend a Jewish school. I asked Mr. Berger why he wasn't worried about pogroms against his grandchildren if people found out that they're Jewish. Father hushed me, but Mr. Berger said that my question was very important. He said there have never been any pogroms against Jews in Canada. Everybody here can practice his religion without any fear. It was so hard for me to even believe that he was telling the truth. Father said he was, but how would Father know? He is new in this country, just like me.

March 13, 1957
4:00 P.M.

I hope my letters will reach you, Sam.

We've just come back from buying boots at the Eaton's department store, as Mr. Berger had suggested.

Like everything else we've done in this country, it turned out to be quite an adventure.

First of all, when we got there we were amazed by the size of the store. We'd never seen one as large before. We had no idea how to find the boots among all the clothes, linen, furniture, and toys that were sold.

"Mr. Berger said that boots might be cheaper downstairs," Mother said in Hungarian. "He said we should ask for . . . oh, how do you say it in English . . . the 'celery'."

Father disagreed with her. "I think he said something else, Kati," he told her.

"Oh, Vili," Mother insisted, "you just don't like to admit that my English is better than yours. Trust me!" Showing supreme confidence, she clasped Ida's hand, put her other arm through Father's arm, and set out for the nearest cosmetics counter. I trotted along behind them.

"Where celery, please?" she asked the saleswoman behind the counter. The woman giggled. A salesman, whose name tag read Manager, hurried over.

"What can I do for you people?"

Mother repeated haughtily, "We looking celery."

The man looked puzzled. "Celery? I think you must want our grocery store on the lower level, madam."

"Not food, no! We want buy boots."

"Celery? Celery? Ah, you must mean cellar. You must be referring to our basement store," the man said, pointing to the escalators leading downstairs.

"I don't know about basement. I want celery for boots," Mother answered, walking away from him with great dignity, with Father and Ida following meekly in her footsteps. I quickly sprayed myself with a sample of Evening in Paris perfume and hurried after her.

All of us found suitable boots. Father was especially fascinated by the slip-on rubbers that fit over the soles and edges of his shoes. They never had those in Hungary.

March 26, 1957
7:00 P.M.

My parents have jobs. And we rented an apartment. Our first home! We'll be moving next week.

Let me tell you about the jobs first. Father has been depressed about not being able to work as a vet. He's been trying to learn English as fast as possible in order to write the same licensing exam as new veterinarians who have just graduated from college. Once he receives his Canadian papers, he'll be able to look for a job as a veterinarian. In the meantime, he goes to daily English classes for new Canadians. He was advised by Canadian veterinarians not to accept any work outside his profession. Mother insisted that he follow their advice, but this led to an argument last week at breakfast.

"It's easy for them to talk," Father said, imitating his Canadian colleagues. "'Go to school, study the language, take your exam as soon as possible.' Who, I would like to know, will put food on the table in the meantime?"

"There is an obvious solution," Mother told him. "I will get a job. You have this idea that I'm totally helpless, just because I was a housewife at home. Don't forget that I have a business degree. I'm still a pretty good typist and bookkeeper."

Father got very red in the face. "I was always able to provide for my family in the past. And I intend to continue to do so in Canada!" My parents never used to fight like this in Hungary. I was very glad when Mother didn't answer him and let the subject drop.

As she cleared the table, Mother announced that she would be out shopping most of the morning. This in itself wasn't unusual, for she buys whatever we need at the door-opening sales to save money. Father is too proud to take advantage of Mr. Berger's generous prices more than necessary.

"The children need new underwear," Mother said to Father.

"I'll come with you, Kati," Father offered. "I need a break from studying."

"No, I'd rather go alone. I can get more done when I'm by myself."

I could see that Father was hurt because they often do the shopping together. When Mother hadn't returned by the afternoon, Father became worried. "Where could your mother be?" he kept repeating, anxiously peering out of the dirty windows of the hotel. It was six o'clock when she finally appeared.

Father was relieved. "Thank goodness you're okay! We thought you may have had an accident," he said to her.

"Vili, girls, I've got something wonderful to tell you. You'll never believe what happened!" Mother said bravely. "I've got a job! You're looking at the newest employee in the Canadian Miss Lingerie Company's accounting department. I'll be working with numbers, so my English won't be a problem."

As Father just stood there silently, all the color drained from his face. Mother's smile quickly faded. "Please, Vili, be happy for me—for us. You know we need the money desperately."

"I'll agree to your working on one condition, Kati," Father finally said. "Ask your boss tomorrow if he has any openings for janitors or machine operators. Don't tell him that I'm a veterinarian, or he'll say that I'm overqualified. Tell him that I was a butcher in Hungary and am really good with my hands."

The next day Father went with Mother to her new job. When he applied for work, the personnel officer could tell by Father's answers that he lacked experience. Father decided to tell him the truth about his professional background and, thank heavens, he was hired as a night watchman. Father loves the job, for it allows him to attend English language classes in the daytime and study for his veterinary exams at night at work. Mother is worried that he is studying too hard and not sleeping enough, but Father is determined to learn English and pass his exams as soon as possible.

Once they were both working, my parents found an apartment right away. I haven't seen it yet, but we'll be moving next week. I can hardly wait to move into our own place. Since our parents started working,

Ida and I have had to stay in the hotel all day. We play cards and try to keep ourselves busy, but I'm going crazy! I'm happy, though, to have a permanent address. I'll write it down at the end of this letter so you can answer my letters. I'm anxious to hear what you've been up to.

Before closing, I've got to tell you about the good-bye party the people at the hotel threw for us last night. Most of the people live here permanently, and we got to know a lot of them. Our special friend is Monsieur Lemieux, a French-Canadian journalist. He is a tall, skeleton-thin man who always has a smelly cigar dangling from his mouth. He loved to tell Ida and me about his adventures as a newspaper corre-spondent during the war. I found his stories interest-ing, even if at times they bored Ida. Sometimes she would hide when she smelled Monsieur Lemieux coming.

The day after Monsieur Lemieux discovered we were going to move, we found a note under our door telling us that he had organized a good-bye party in our honor for the following evening. When we walked down to the hotel lobby, we found the room decorated with crêpe-paper streamers and a card-board sign wishing us good luck. It was hard to rec-ognize our fellow guests in their Sunday clothes. Monsieur Lemieux even prepared fruit punch and bought a cake from the bakery. There were party hats for all of us. My parents and Ida looked so ridiculous when they put them on that I refused to wear mine, despite Mother's teasing. A record player was blaring in the corner. It wasn't Elvis Presley singing, but another singer called Frank Sinatra. We all had so much fun that the party didn't break up until midnight. Before we went back to our room, Monsieur Lemieux gave both Ida and me a box of chocolates. And Mrs. Jennings, the oldest of the chambermaids, gave us her collection of cards with pictures of flowers on them. These cards were prizes in boxes of tea. She must have drunk hundreds of cups of tea to gather such a large collection.

So you see, Sam, that while I'm happy to be moving to our own apartment, I'm also sad to leave the Hotel Darlington.

Well, I guess I should finish this letter now. I bet it's the longest letter you have ever received. Perhaps I should become a writer when I grow up!

I hope you'll reply soon. I want to hear all about your adventures in Winnipeg. My new address is:

    102-999 Bernard Ave.
    Montreal, Quebec, Canada

Thinking of you,
Nelly

P. S. Do you miss me?

14

Our Apartment

I was terribly disappointed when I saw our new apartment for the first time. It was a dark, grim place in the basement of an old brownstone. The walls were covered in striped gray wallpaper yellowed with age and stained with watermarks. The window coverings were tattered blinds, grimy with years of neglect. There was only one bedroom but, after living in a single room, the apartment seemed vast to me. Ida and I would share the room and my parents would sleep on a pull-out couch in the living room. Before we moved, we had bought some used furniture—an old tweed couch in a nauseating mustard shade, a wobbly wooden coffee table, an old kitchen set with four mismatched chairs, and two army-style iron beds. We also bought heavy, white dishes, some cutlery, and bedding, including rough, gray blankets that became our window drapes in the daytime. The only piece of furniture I liked was the old TV set in a corner of the living room.

I was trying to be considerate and helpful, but I couldn't stop myself from complaining to Mother while I helped her set the kitchen table for supper. "My new blanket is so prickly! I hate to cover myself with it," I whined. "As soon as it touches my skin, I'm itchy all over. I won't use it! I'd rather freeze to death!"

"It's up to you, but you'll be cold then, Nelly."

Ida, who had been growing more cheerful every day, suddenly began to cry. "I want my room at home. I don't like it here." I was surprised to feel tears running down my own face.

"Let's sit down," Mother said. She pulled out one of the rickety chairs by the kitchen table. We sat down beside her. She looked at each of us in turn very seriously, and clasped our hands between hers. "You're no longer babies," she told us. "Enough self-pity! You've got to accept that this apartment is our home now. There's no looking back. I miss my furniture and dishes whenever I see these ugly plates and this cutlery," she said, pointing to the table. "I promise you, as soon as Father passes his examination and gets a job in his profession, we'll have nice things. But you've got to be more patient. In the meantime, we're better off here, in our own place, than in a hotel room. And Janos, Maria, and David live five minutes away. We'll be able to see them all the time." She looked at us with a smile on her lips, but it was not reflected in her eyes.

Ida looked at me and rolled her eyes. I winked back to signal that this wasn't the time to tell Mother again how we felt about David. "You're right," I said. "We'll soon get used to living here, won't we, Ida?"

Ida's lips were pressed together in a stubborn expression. She didn't answer. "We'll soon like living here, won't we?" I repeated in a pointed tone.

Ida nodded reluctantly. "I'll get Jutka," she said. "She hasn't seen the apartment yet."

"What a good idea." Mother stood up. "I still have a lot to do. Nelly, can you help me unpack our suitcase? It shouldn't take long."

Although we had very few possessions, it was eight o'clock in the evening before everything was in its place. The new apartment was full of shadowy corners and strange noises. The constant hum of the furnace and the refrigerator seemed loud and unwelcoming. Even the furniture seemed out of place, grouped like a crowd of strangers waiting for a train.

I watched Father sitting on the couch. Today was his day off from work. A newspaper was spread open but remained unread on his lap. He was a million miles away, gazing into the air, lost in thought.

Mother was at the kitchen table engrossed in her precious photographs. I walked over, pulled up a chair, and took her hand. She glanced up startled, and shook her head as if to rid it of cobwebs.

"What are you doing?" I asked her.

"Oh, I was thinking how strange life can be. What would my parents say if they could see us in this apartment, in this frozen land so far from home?" She sighed deeply and wrapped her arm around my shoulders. "You know, before the war my father used to save all of my toys when I became too old for them. He said he wanted them for his grandchildren. My mother never used her best embroidered tablecloths. She put them away so that I could use them when I got married and had my own home." She sighed again and smoothed out the folds in the plastic tablecover.

"Come on, Mother, you said that we had to be patient. We're better off here than in a hotel." I repeated back to her exactly what she had said to us earlier.

"You're right, this is home now." She brightened up. "Thank heaven I remembered to bring my pictures with me. As soon as I can, I'll buy frames for them. Would you like one of them for your room? You can pick the one you want."

I pointed to my favorite—my mother as a little girl standing between her parents. "I'll go to my room to decide where to hang it," I told her. She beamed at me in reply.

Ida was crouching in a corner, arranging the shoebox that served as her doll's crib. Jutka herself was already tucked into Ida's bed, her sleepless eyes blankly staring into the shabby room. I thought of the original Jutka sitting on another bed, her china-blue eyes wide open, guarding our empty room and futilely waiting for our return.

Suddenly, I didn't feel like picking a spot for Mother's photograph. I would decide where to put it tomorrow. I got undressed and crawled into bed, my mind full of thoughts of my room at home—the comfortable armchairs, the warmth of the ceramic stove, the lace curtains filtering the sunlight. I remembered my books and the velvet dress I had worn only once. I remembered Sari coming over after school and Miki dancing with me at my birthday party. It all seemed so long ago, so far away. I turned my face into my pillow and allowed myself to quietly cry until I fell asleep.

15

Gladstone School

For the first time in four months, Ida and I would be going to school. I longed to be with other children, but I was worried that I wouldn't be able to understand them. Even worse, what if they couldn't understand me?

"Everything will be fine," Father tried to reassure me. "It's time that the two of you got some order back into your lives. Your English is good, and you can make yourself understood without a great deal of difficulty. Mother will go with you tomorrow morning because it's the first day but, after that, you're on your own. Isn't it lucky there are eight grades in your new school? You'll be able to keep an eye on Ida."

"Sure, Father, I'll keep an eye on her," I promised, earning a smile from him.

"Father and I have a surprise for you," Mother announced. She went to the closet and pulled out two hangers with navy tunics and crisp white blouses on them. "These are the uniforms you'll wear." Even though we would be attending public school, we would be required to wear uniforms.

The uniforms fit us perfectly and looked rather nice. The tunic style, pleated from the square neck and worn with a belt made of the same material, made me look slimmer. Ida, as always, was a little stick, but she didn't care as long as her clothes were comfortable. Mother also bought us matching navy stockings and polished our scuffed brown oxfords so well that I could see my face in them. When I looked in the mirror a smiling stranger was staring back at me. In her uniform, she looked just like any other Canadian girl on her way to school.

A blistering wind chilled us to the bone as we picked our way through piles of snow in the yard of Gladstone School. The school was an ugly, gray stone building, three stories high with a curving fire escape hugging the left wall. It was so different from my school on top of the hill at home. A large arrow on a sign by the main entrance directed us to the office of the principal, Miss Green. I had to gulp down a laugh when I first saw her. She looked like a cartoon schoolteacher. She was very tall, with her graying hair screwed into a tight topknot and kind but shrewd eyes peering out from behind her horn-rimmed glasses. She listened attentively to Mother's fragmented explanation of our past schooling, and she spoke to us very slowly, so we had no difficulty understanding her.

"So, Mrs. Adler, what you're telling me is that the children didn't attend any school at all for the last four months and, prior to that, Nelly was in grade seven and Ida in grade four for only two months at the beginning of the school year in Hungary."

"Yes. Correct." Mother said, "My husband and me think good idea to put the girls back a year. Proper grades while learning English may be hard for them." Surely I had misunderstood what Mother was trying to say. Was she actually proposing that Ida and I lose a year? No wonder she didn't have the nerve to discuss this plan with us at home. She must have known how upset we would be at such a suggestion.

"I do wish that you had some of the children's records with you, Mrs. Adler, but I understand the situation. We already have four other Hungarian refugee students attending our school, and we enrolled all of them a grade behind what they attended in Hungary to make their adjustment to the Canadian school system easier."

I opened my mouth to protest, but no sound came out. Ida leaned over to me and whispered, "Do something! This isn't fair."

I realized that I had to get hold of myself and speak up. I finally managed to croak, "Can I ask you something?"

"Nelly, your manners! Don't interrupt principal!" Mother exclaimed.

"It's quite all right, Mrs. Adler," the principal said. "I encourage children to speak for themselves. What do you want to ask me, Nelly?"

I was very careful with my reply. A lot was riding on it. I took a deep breath, and plunged right in. "Could you please . . ." Oh, what was the proper English word I wanted to use? I just couldn't think of it. But the idea of walking into a class as an outsider, much less an outsider who towered over everyone, was a strong spur.

"Take your time, Nelly," the principal said. I noticed that her eyes were regarding me kindly behind her thick glasses.

I began again. "Ida and me want to be in same grade in Canada as in Hungary. We're best students in school in Hungary. We work very hard." I finally ran out of steam and stopped talking. Ida squeezed my hand in approval.

Miss Green was in deep thought, biting her lip while she considered my proposal. "Okay," she finally said, "let's give it a try. I'll put you in grade seven, Nelly, and Ida in grade four until Easter, and then we'll review the situation. If you can't keep up with your classmates, you'll be moved back a year. Is that fair?"

"Very fair, thank you," I told her. Ida was smiling from ear to ear. Mother nodded her agreement.

"Well, that's settled then," Miss Green said. "I'm glad to see that both girls already have uniforms. Younger children must wear their uniforms all the time, but the grade sevens and eights can be in their own clothes on Fridays. The dress code is strictly enforced. As for lunch, it's from noon to one-thirty. Most students bring their lunch to school, but perhaps today you'd like the girls to go home for lunch?" she asked Mother.

"Oh no, we don't have to," I told her, "Mother packed us sandwiches."

"Well then, it seems we're all organized," Miss Green said, standing up from her desk. "I'll take you to your classrooms. Classes end at three-thirty, Mrs. Adler," she continued. I could see that her decisive manner had reassured Mother. With hurried thanks and an encouraging wink to us, Mother was gone.

"Come on," the principal summoned us, "let's go to your classrooms. Ida, your teacher's name is Mrs. Williams, and you'll be in Mr. Robertson's homeroom, Nelly."

The class was hushed as I followed Miss Green into the grade seven room on the second floor. I could actually feel everyone's eyes boring into me.

"We have a new addition to your room, Mr. Robertson," Miss Green announced in hearty tones. "Nelly Adler comes to us from Hungary. I hope that all of you will welcome her and help her to get used to our ways here." My heart was thumping so loudly I was sure everyone could hear it.

"Welcome to Canada and to our class," said Mr. Robertson in a loud voice. Somebody stifled a snicker in the back of the room. I could feel the heat rising to my face. "Please God, let them like me," I prayed silently.

"Quiet," Mr. Robertson said as he led me to a desk between a pretty girl with long, curly brown hair and a red-headed boy. "Marni," Mr. Robertson said to the girl, "I'd like you to look after Nelly and show her how we do things in our school. There aren't any empty lockers available. Would you mind sharing yours with her?"

She agreed and then turned to me and smiled as if she really meant it. The sprinkling of fine freckles over the bridge of her nose reminded me of Sari back in Hungary. A sudden longing for my old class and friends overwhelmed me for a moment, but then I told myself not to be silly and tried to concentrate on what Mr. Robertson was saying.

"Thank you, Marni," he said. "Perhaps you could give Nelly a tour of the school over lunch hour. Nelly," he added, turning to me, "if you need any extra help, please don't hesitate to ask me. Do you have any questions?"

"My English very bad," I told the teacher.

"I'll be holding special language classes three times a week for our new foreign students. You'll be amazed how quickly your English will improve," Mr. Robertson said. The bell rang just then, signaling the beginning of lunch-hour.

Marni was very helpful. She gave me a copy of the timetable and explained that we had to go to different classrooms for different subjects. We had Mr. Robertson for math and science, Mr. Hall for social studies and art, and Miss Smith for language arts and gym. We toured the school. It was at least twice the size of my school back home. I asked where Ida's classroom was located, but Ida was not there. Marni pointed out the washrooms and the lockers. Then she and I went to the lunchroom, where we joined some other girls from our class. Ida was sitting at a table with some of the younger children. She was laughing, so everything must have been going well for her. I tried to follow the conversation at my table, but the English words whirled around me until I felt that I was drowning in words. The girls were talking about a TV show all of them had seen the night before. It was called "The Ed Sullivan Show". I'd never heard of it.

I looked up and saw the red-haired boy who sat next to me in class coming down the staircase leading into the lunchroom.

"Hey, Rob, come on over," called out a plump girl with black hair. I didn't know her name yet. He waved to her and headed for our table. "Do you want to sit with us?" she asked, moving over to make room for him.

"No," he answered, "it stinks too much here." He pinched his nose with his thumb and forefinger. "Where is this stink coming from?" he asked. He pretended to look around the table and to notice me for the first time. He took a step backward, apparently astonished to see me. "That explains it," he said, "you're sitting with the DP. All DPS stink."

There was sudden silence at our table. A tall girl named Rachel giggled. "You're right," she said. "Yuck! Let's move." Why was everybody looking at me? Were they talking about me? Maybe I should have spoken up and explained to them that I took a bath every day. But it didn't matter. All of them moved to another table and the opportunity was gone. Only Marni and I remained. She unwrapped her sandwich. It was peanut butter and jelly. I opened my lunch. Mother had packed me a slice of dark rye bread with a thick layer of butter and green peppers on top.

"Do you want to trade?" Marni asked. Her smile was just like Sari's back home.

"Yes, I'd like," I stammered.

"You should have told those idiots to shut up," Marni said.

"I didn't know they talk about me at first, then it too late. What's a DP?"

"Oh, nothing," she said. "They're stupid. Forget it."

"No, please, tell me."

"A DP is a displaced person, somebody who doesn't have a country, doesn't have a home. Don't listen to them. You've got a country. Canada is your country now."

I couldn't speak. I clenched my teeth to stop myself from breaking into tears. Just then, the bell rang, marking the end of the lunch-hour.

"Hurry up," Marni said, careful not to look at me, "or we'll be late for class." I followed her silently out of the room, still shaken.

It took forever for school to end. Except for Amy, the girl with the black hair, who asked my name in math class, only Marni talked to me the entire day. Rob knocked my books off my desk in both math and social studies class, claiming that it was an accident. But I got the idea. My facial muscles were sore from fighting the tears that had threatened to fall all day. Marni waited for me at the end of classes to walk home together. Ida had already left with one of her new friends. Several classmates passed us, but nobody joined us. Marni's face was red with anger.

"You don't have to walk with me," I told her. "Then others go with you."

"Don't be silly, Nelly. I want to walk with you. Let's go back to your apartment. I want to see your room."

Suddenly, I heard footsteps behind us. It was Rob and four other boys from our grade.

"Ignore them," Marni said.

Rob and his friends surrounded us and blocked our path. "Go home, DP!" they chanted. "Go home! We don't want you here. Go away!"

"Get away from us, or I'll tell Miss Green," Marni cried.

"Goody two-shoes. DP lover!" Rob said to her.

"Shut up, creep," Marni said, snarling. "Get out of our way!"

I felt paralyzed. I couldn't move. I couldn't speak. I didn't know what to do. There were so many of them and only one of me. If I opened my mouth, they would only make more fun of me. Perhaps if I didn't answer back, they would get sick of bothering me and just leave. I searched my brain frantically for what the old Nelly would have done, but my mind drew a blank. The old Nelly had vanished.

"Get out of our way, or you'll be sorry in a big way!" Marni threatened, and they finally let us go.

I could hear them until we turned the corner at the end of the street, still yelling after us in a poor imitation of my Hungarian accent. "DP go home! DP go home! We don't want you here!"

There was nowhere else for me to go. I wished there was.

Time passed quickly. We had been at Gladstone School for two months and my English had improved. Schoolwork in Canada was much easier than at home. I had been getting top marks in my class in every subject, except language arts. Whenever Mr. Robertson distributed tests he had marked he always announced, "As usual, Nelly got one hundred per cent." I wished I had the nerve to ask him not to praise me so much, because every day after school Rob and his friends followed a few steps behind me all the way home, screaming at the top of their lungs in a fake Hungarian accent, "Huuundred, huuundred!"

Marni walked home with me, and acted as if Rob and his buddies didn't exist. "Pretend they're not there. They're idiots," she said. "They're jealous because you're smarter than they are."

Marni couldn't be telling me the whole truth. There had to be some other reason why these children hated me so. Was it because I spoke with an accent? Not all people look alike, so why should they all sound alike? In the mornings when I brushed my teeth, I studied my face in the mirror. I looked like I used to in Hungary, yet in Veszprem I had lots of friends. Why didn't my Canadian classmates like me? Something had to be wrong with me, or they would like me at least a little bit. My reflection told me nothing. The same Nelly stared back at me day after day. What was wrong with me? I had to find out somehow. I couldn't tell my parents what was happening to me at school. They expected me to be happy. Also, their Hungarian accents were much more pronounced than mine. With time, Rob's taunts became my private shame, a secret that had to be kept at all costs from my parents. Even Ida, who told Mother everything, knew better than to mention to her what had been happening to me at school.

Ida was having a much easier time than me. She was learning to speak English without an accent, and had lots of friends in her class. I watched her during recess jumping rope and skipping around the schoolyard arm in arm with other little girls. Younger children in Canada seemed to be friendlier. Ida didn't need me anymore.

Well, at least I had Marni. We spent a lot of time together after school. She was also Jewish, and asked me to come with her to religion classes at the synagogue on Sunday mornings. Nobody in Canada seemed to care what religion people practiced. I wondered what the other children would say if I told them about pogroms and other experiences I had had in Europe? No use telling them. They wouldn't be interested in anything I had to say. Marni was my only friend. She said it was up to me to show the other students that I was friendly, and encouraged me to take the first step. But why should I? They didn't care about me.

One day after school, I mustered all my courage to ask Marni a question. "Be honest with me, Marni. Why does everybody in our class hate me? What's wrong with me?" I couldn't bear to meet her eyes, but I had to know.

"Don't be silly. They don't hate you. And nothing's wrong with you," Marni said too quickly. I knew her well enough by now to be certain that she was keeping something from me.

"Tell me the truth," I pressed her. "I know they don't like me. But why? What's wrong with me?"

"Okay, I'll tell you. But remember, you made me," Marni said with a pained look on her face. "You're different from the rest of us, Nelly. It's not only your accent.

It's everything. You think differently; you act differently; and you look different. This is most noticeable on Fridays, when we're not required to wear our uniforms. And your pigtails, well, nobody in the whole grade has braids except for you."

I could feel the heat rising in my cheeks. Had everybody noticed that I had been wearing the same shapeless navy skirt every week? They must all have been laughing at me. It hurt to know.

"I wouldn't pay any attention to anybody in our class," Marni said. "Ignore them."

"Tell me what else they say," I insisted.

"Just forget about them."

"I can't. Tell me."

"They say you look weird—like you just stepped off the boat," Marni said reluctantly.

I turned my head away so she wouldn't see the tears welling up in my eyes. I *had* just stepped off the boat.

Mother appeared at the door. "What's going on? What's wrong?" she asked with a frown when she saw my face.

"Nothing," I told her.

"I'm going to tell your mother," Marni said.

"Don't you dare!"

"I've got to. Maybe she can help."

Mother ushered us inside and Marni explained to her what had been happening to me at school. I was relieved that she didn't bring up how Rob made fun of the way I spoke English. I turned my back on them and stared fixedly out of the window.

Mother was silent for a long moment. I concentrated

on the buzzing of a fly trying to find a way to get outside of the window pane. Mother let out a shuddering sigh. "I had no idea. . . . Although I wondered why nobody but you, Marni . . . Well, never mind. Let's see what we can do. So, Marni," Mother asked, "what do you think we can do to help the situation?"

"I think it might help Nelly if she felt as if she fit in better. I don't think that most of our classmates dislike Nelly. It's just that some of them don't know how to react if anybody is different from them. And, even though she's never said anything to me, I think Nelly feels self-conscious because her clothes and her hair make her feel that she is not like the rest of us."

"Do you think that if Nelly gets some new clothes and cuts her hair, she might have an easier time fitting in?"

"It might help her feel like less of an outsider," Marni said.

"It sounds as if it's time we went shopping for a new wardrobe for you, Nelly." Mother turned to me with a smile.

"You know we can't afford anything now!"

"Let me be the judge of what we can afford," Mother said sternly. "What do you need the most?"

"She should have saddle shoes and a leather jacket for spring. All the girls are wearing plaid skirts and mohair sweaters," Marni said. She was describing her own outfit.

"Good! What else?" Mother asked, turning to me. "Are you going to let Marni pick all your clothes for you?"

"I also need a new blouse and a belt. My old one is too

small," I replied. I was starting to get excited, but I was trying not to show it.

"It all sounds reasonable to me," Mother said. "Tomorrow is Saturday, so we can take the bus to Simpsons-Sears and buy what you need. We'd appreciate your advice, Marni. And, Nelly, after we finish shopping, you can get your hair cut."

We arrived at the department store early the next morning. Mother bought me two plaid skirts, in purple and brown patterns, and blue and white cotton blouses. Marni noticed a pink mohair cardigan hanging on the rack.

She held it out for me. "Try it on, it's beautiful." I ran my hands over the sleeves. Then I slipped my arms into the sweater. The mohair tickled my nose and felt prickly and itchy against my neck, but it looked so nice on me that Mother said she would buy it for me. I remembered the velvety softness of the party dress I had left behind in Hungary, but I decided I liked this sweater much more than my European clothes.

We found saddle shoes and a white vinyl jacket that looked just like real leather. There were even identical wide patent leather belts for Marni and me. Marni didn't want to accept the gift, but she discovered that if Mother made up her mind she wouldn't take no for an answer. The belt made my waist look small and the skirt billowed out in a most satisfactory manner when I pirouetted in front of the mirror. The saleslady put my old clothes in a bag when Mother paid for my new outfits.

"You look so nice, " Marni said with a wide smile on her face.

"Very pretty indeed," Mother added. "But now it's time to visit the beauty shop on the first floor."

The thought of having my hair cut petrified me. I had been growing my braids for the last seven years, and they were a part of me, like my arms and legs. I couldn't look when the hairdresser snipped them off. My eyes stayed tightly closed as he shaped the rest of my hair. Finally, Mother told me to open my eyes. A Canadian stranger with my features looked back at me from the mirror. My head felt light, as if it were floating. My face was framed by soft, brown curls that emphasized my cheekbones and brown eyes. I wished that Sam could see me now.

16

Home

"Nelly, come and help me set the table," Mother called. We were having a special Canadian meal of hamburgers and french fries tonight in celebration of Father passing his veterinary exams.

I pretended not to hear her calling me because I had important things to discuss with Marni. We were sitting in the cozy room I shared with Ida. Ida was at a friend's house, so Marni and I had the room to ourselves. She was perched on the threadbare but comfortable blue armchair under the window, and I was sitting on one of the two army-style iron beds we got from the HIAS. I automatically smoothed down my skirt under my legs before sitting down because I was wearing ankle socks. As soon as the backs of my thighs rubbed against the rough, gray blanket I broke out in an ugly red rash.

I looked around my room at the objects that were now familiar to me. There was the rickety dresser with a round mirror above it. Next to the mirror hung the photograph of my mother as a little girl. An old desk and chair were beside my bed. The bookshelf above the desk held my treasures—the shell bracelet I wore on special occasions, the taped-up copy of *Toldi*, the English version of *Twenty Thousand Leagues Under the Sea* Marni had given me, and an old cookie tin that held my letters from Sam. Mother had sewed pretty drapes out of flower-patterned sheets for the window. The sun cast a golden floral glow on the walls as it filtered through them.

"Do you want to play Monopoly?" Marni asked.

"No, let's decide what we'll do this weekend."

Marni looked away. "I made some plans already," she said. "A couple of girls from our class are going to the matinee to see *Around the World in Eighty Days*. Come with us. It's supposed to be a funny movie."

"It is. I read the book in Hungary. But you go ahead without me. Your friends don't want me to come along or they would have already asked me. . . ."

"You're too sensitive, Nelly," Marni said. "You have to take the first step. You have to show people how terrific you are."

I walked over to the bookshelf and fiddled with my bracelet to stall for time. I pulled it onto my wrist. The tiny shells tinkled when I moved my hand. I remembered how happy I had been when Father bought it for me aboard the ship bringing us to Canada.

The shell bracelet brought back a lot of memories. It reminded me of the gold ring I had given to the Hungarian soldiers to get them to help us cross the border to Austria. It also reminded me of my beautiful shell collection, sitting on a bookshelf in a faraway room with lace-patterned shadows. It reminded me of Miki, of Sari, the overturned gravestones, and my birthday party. It brought back the sight of Father with blood running down his face when he was interrogated by the Russian soldiers. It reminded me of Eva, of *Toldi* and the immigrant camps, of Sam and the *Venezuela*. It reminded me of my first day of school in Canada, when I felt I would drown in words I couldn't understand. It reminded me of my classmates chanting "DP go home!" I glanced around my room, shabby but now familiar and beloved. I was home.

I squared my shoulders and faced Marni. She was smiling at me with encouragement. I gulped down past hurts, past fears.

"You're right," I told her. "I'll come with you. It's time they got to know me."